I'M THE PRESIDENT, BY DONALD THUMP

A book of fiction, perhaps

By

George A.M. Heroux

Strategic Book Publishing and Rights Co.

Strategic Book Publishing and Rights Co., LLC
USA | Singapore
www.sbpra.com

For information about special discounts for bulk purchases, please contact Strategic Book Publishing and Rights Co. Special Sales, at bookorder@sbpra.net.

ISBN: 978-1-950015-05-4

Table of Contents

Prologue

I have to tell you that this is one of those tell-all books. It's doubtful that there is a priest who would listen to my confession, so my readers, here is that recounting of deeds being told directly to you. The tell-all aspect features me more than others. After all, that's my favorite subject. I started writing this book right after I was elected President of the United States and continued working on it during my Presidency. Now, it's going into a vault to be released after I am living in a part of the world where no one can touch me. I suppose that some people will just call it a diary because I recounted deeds as they occurred, but this is no diary; it's a book with solid historical information and an opportunity for the reader to know the real me.

I have many friends, although I would guess that some people don't like me. Most of those who would rather spit at me than smile at me are the envious ones. There is no way that any of them could have or will reach my financial or power status. You have no doubt heard of me. I'm Donald Thump.

Topic 1: Business Beginnings

It all started humbly enough. My father made a few bucks in real estate and I thought why not join the family business. The thing is I had no interest in hanging onto his coattails. I was determined to make it on my own. Me, me, me. That's when I bought my first apartment building, a 24-unit in a run-down area of town: Title-Eightsville.

Making money in commercial property is not rocket science. You buy the property for the minimum amount down, use whatever government funds are out there for back-up, and with credit obtained using someone else's guarantee (my father). The price you pay has to be negotiated with the seller to an amount that will require mortgage payments way below the rentals you collect. You buy the property in an area that's sure to improve because you've had inside information from a local government official that the city is going to spend serious money to improve the area. What the heck, even if you do nothing to improve the apartments that you buy, the value goes up because the value of property around you has increased. Of course, you don't want to waste any money on making life better for your tenants. I suppose some of the jealous people would call me a slum landlord.

Of course you don't want to stay with that property forever. No, no. A few years down the road you have garnered some serious equity. Then you sell to some sucker who thinks he can make a go of it, but you sell it for a whole lot more than it's worth. And of course, you don't pay any taxes on the sale because you buy another property pursuant to a tax provision that allows a tax-free exchange. Naturally, while you own the property, you are depreciating it for tax purposes for a loss against any other income you have.

Let me say a bit about the renters as illustrated in this conversation with the prior owner, a guy named Barry Lapes.

Me: What the make-up of the tenants, racially I mean?

Barry: We've got some Blacks, some Hispanics, a few Puerto Ricans, one Chinese family. No Whites.

Me: All Title Eights?

Barry: No, no. Some of these folks can afford the rent, just don't want to spend their money on shelter. Know what I mean?

Me: Yeah, that's fine, as long as they pay the rent on time.

Barry: Oh, yeah. If they don't, I got a lawyer who gets them out pronto.

Me: Good policy.

The guy thought he was pretty slick, but I knew he wanted to unload. It wasn't that difficult to get him to bail out for a bargain price.

Eventually, I stepped up to much better properties. Then, of course, I kept out the riffraff. You know what I mean. I was pretty careful about keeping up the value of the properties with the right tenants.

You know, because of where I am now, I don't mind sharing some secrets. You get rich by using what the laws in this country give you and by taking advantage of people who aren't as smart as you are. That means you zero in on the least brightest and you use the tax code and bankruptcy laws in the blink of an eye.

I'll give you an example. I got into the craze of gambling when the state allowed slots in strip shopping centers. Before then, you had to go to a casino, sometimes at a distance. I placed fifty of those babies. Made it big for a while, splashed my name, Thump, on every one of them. A lot of suckers out there, so I took in some serious coin. But, like all good things, the action cooled. That was the first time I used bankruptcy as an out. That was my first association with a bankruptcy lawyer, Johnnie Macon.

Me: I don't know, Johnnie, I feel a little guilty about stiffing the bank and credit card companies.

Johnnie: Hey, what do you think they're doing to you? The enormous interest rates that you've been paying reap in big-time profits for them and pay for all the expected no-pays.

Me: You mean guys like me, entrepreneurs, are expected not to pay sometimes?

Johnnie: Exactly. Anyway, you set up this L.L.C. to avoid personal liability, didn't you? If they were stupid enough to loan money to your company without your personal guaranty, they deserve to be screwed.

Me: Yeah, I guess. Okay, let's do it.

Don't get me wrong. Bankruptcy was rare for me. Most of the time, I hit it big. Got into business properties. Six or seven times I built office buildings for state agencies. Once again, it sure paid to have friends on the inside. There was Sal. What a guy. He gave me the lead on the first one.

Sal: Yeah, our agency's thinking about a facility that's going to cover half a block, a couple hundred offices.

Me: I'd be interested in putting that project together for you guys.

Sal: You're not alone. Of course, I'm in the position to steer it your way if, maybe, you're inclined to sweeten the deal.

Me: That sounds illegal to me, Sal, but I'm not a fanatic about sticking to the exact letter of the law.

That's how my government building began. The deal was fantastic, so good that I could pick the lender from among many suitors. We locked in 50-year lease contracts. Hell, the buildings were paid for in ten years. All gravy after that. Anyway, I'll tell you more about my business ventures later in the book.

Topic 2: Russia

What's with everyone's concern about Russia? People accuse me of cozying up to Gobashitzen. Why not turn a potential enemy into a friend? Look at history. We fought the British, didn't we? Now they're our buddies. We fought Germany twice in the 20th Century. Now we have a great relationship with that country. Japan attacked us. Now we count on the Japanese economy to keep our stocks at a comfortable level. It's time to get along with Russia.

Andrei Gobashitzen is a good guy. As everyone knows, I have companies that have done very well in dealings with Russia during his tenure. I've met with him personally a half dozen times, but we decided not to reveal that fact during the campaign. I remember my first conversation with him.

Gobashitzen: Donald, you're an excellent businessman. My country has numerous businesses that would do well to develop commercial activity with some of your companies.

Me: I have international interests and I like the Russian people. I believe them to be hardy and industrious. I've met with some of them informally. I have nothing but good things to say about them.

Gobashitzen: I feel that way about you Americans. I just don't understand how we drifted into that cold war after we cooperated so well during World War II. Sure, we have different forms of government. Why should that prevent two such glorious countries from working together for the good of all?

Me: My feelings exactly. Thank you for setting up meetings for me with some of your best industries. My money and your resources go well together, I believe.

Gobashitzen: Absolutely. Let your Congressmen moan and groan about our very practical partnership. They are living in the past. You and I are the future, Donald.

Russia is certainly not the scary place it used to be. There is no reason to fear its leaders. They realize that only good will come from a tight partnership in global affairs. There is no question that we must be aware of our responsibilities as world leaders. We have the military power and economic resources to wipe out every other country in the world, so intervention in hotspot situations everywhere has to be of interest to both countries. The past has demonstrated how those powers were exercised, sometimes by guile or diplomacy, sometimes by military necessities.

It appears often that Russia has its own agenda and, in the past, has not consulted the United States about global matters. I intend to put all that aside. If Russia moves without consultation with us in matters that involve European, Asian, or Middle Eastern matters, I believe that we can sway them with direct communication. Whatever happened to that direct line between the President and the Soviet leader? We're going to make sure that phone is in constant operation between the two leaders so that we can discuss those issues. I believe that the Russian government and the Russian people want peace. I think that now that we have two clear-thinking individuals running these countries, we'll see never-before-seen harmony.

The very first thing that we have to do is wipe out that threat to humanity: ICES. Russia agrees with me on this one. No doubt. We've been bombing them selectively. Russia agrees that we need an all-out effort by both of our governments. That effort may include using our nuclear arsenal. That scares many of our old thinkers. I believe that we can use nuclear weapons whenever there is good reason to do so. I think that we have to be very careful about deciding when to use them, but if the need is great, I say KABOOM. Gobas agrees with me. We are going to issue a joint statement that tells ICES: Disband or get the crap nuclear bombed out of you.

I know that using nuclear weapons will not be popular among those who fear proliferation. They claim that the use of these weapons would be the beginning of the end of the world, that everyone with nuclear capability will want to join the party. Hell, one devastating attack by a joint effort of Russia and the United States would scare everyone else into submission. I discussed this fully with Gobas a few weeks after I took office.

Gobashitzen: Donald, now that we are seeing eye to eye, we must seize upon the opportunity to work together to remove the bad guys from this world. I love that term bad guys. I got it from listening to your classic radio shows on SiriusXM radio.

Me: I loved those shows too. Ever hear of the Lone Ranger? He's my favorite.

Gobashitzen: Oh yes, and The Shadow too. (Imitates the lead-in) Who knows what evil lurks in the hearts of men? The Shadow knows, ha, ha, ha.

Me: We certainly can learn from those old heroes. They wouldn't hesitate to use whatever is at their disposal to bring about law and order. That's what we must do.

The last time I met with Gobas was early in the Presidential campaign. He was concerned that my opponent, Helen Haze, would defeat me in the general election.

Gobashitzen: Is there any way that we can assist you in your efforts to become the next American President?

Me: Oh, no, I don't believe that you should be interfering in our election. Having said that, let me ask you. What did you have in mind?

Gobashitzen: I hesitate to brag but I must tell you that we have excellent hacking abilities. It may be that we could add an email here or there, eliminate a few, altar the meaning of some of them. That kind of thing. Also, we're pretty adept at making moves on social media.

Me: It is true that much of the good work that you and I can do working together would certainly never take place if Senator Haze won the election, but no, no, you can't do that. Well, at least if you do, I don't want to know about it.

Gobashitzen: Well, then, we won't interfere. Not much. Ha, ha, ha.

I don't think that Russia ever did interfere with our very democratic election by hacking emails, but I'm sure not going to worry about it. I have instructed my techie folks to make sure it doesn't happen in the future. What happened in the past will just stay in the past.

Oh, yeah, Gobas had some other ideas about winning. He is a fierce competitor, no doubt.

Gobashitzen: You know, Donald, we use other methods sometimes to assure that we get what we want.

Me: You mean whatever is necessary.

Gobashitzen: Exactly. In my own life I've had to see to it that things happen, maybe bribery, maybe physical harm, maybe, as they say in your Godfather movies, "sleep with the fishes."

Me: I don't think I want to know about those activities, but I understand your leadership is very competitive and sometimes you must engage in certain behavior that is not common in the United States.

Gobashitzen: Well, my friend, don't worry about your back. I've got it.

Topic 3: Guns

I'm a strong advocate of the Second Amendment to the United States Constitution. I believe that the best way to protect ourselves from the scum of this country is to have everyone armed to the teeth. Yes, not only one gun per person but I would encourage every American citizen to build an arsenal of weapons. I heard a comedian on television one night say that the best way to avoid air jacking is make sure that everyone on the plane has a gun. If they don't have one when they get on the plane, the comedian said, hand them one. I'm not so sure that the guy didn't have something.

The need for arming everyone is evident. Look at Chicago. Seems like a half dozen people get shot every day in that city. The thing is it's the bad guys who have the guns. If people started shooting back, there would be fewer murders and a number of self-defense killings. If that happens often enough, just maybe we can put an end to this murder epidemic.

It's true that the National Rifle Association was very generous in contributing to my campaign. They weren't trying to influence my thinking on gun control; they already knew about my love for guns in the hands of the right people. That Charlton Heston was an upright guy. I remember one of my conversations with NRA leader Clint (Shoot now, talk later) Rellik.

Rellik: Donald, we know that you believe in the right of Americans to own and use guns when necessary. You know, though, don't you, that we manufacture guns for the sportsman and for police use? It is simply a bonus that guns are used for protection and for doing the right thing at the right time.

Me: If you could only prevent those terrible tragedies, those school shootings and mass shootings in public places.

Rellik: We can, we can. In every one of those situations, if everyone had a gun, the mass shooters would be blasted before they did too much damage.

Me: You know I pack one. If the time ever comes when I need this baby, I'm going to fire away.

Rellik: We would like to make you a present of our newest rapid-fire weapon. This guy fires five shots a second. The bullets are especially made for this gun; they can penetrate armor. Ain't nobody gonna survive a blast from this beauty.

Me: Can you imagine the look of surprise on anybody threatening you with a pistol when you pull this monster out of your concealed weapon holster?

Rellik: Sure, just before he hits the dust.

Me: I'll accept your gift. You understand that I can't endorse your products, don't you?

Rellik: Oh, yeah, yeah. Listen, we have another small gift for you, a check for your campaign expenses, $80-million.

The way I look at it, supporting an amendment to the U.S. constitution is about American as you can get. Those are the guys I want supporting me. I back the NRA because, in the long run, the NRA will save lives. Whether it's a 38 special stub nose or a gun that spits bullets, gun manufacturers should continue to provide guns that do the job without interference from government. What do I mean by interference? Dictating the kinds of guns that are legal, making it difficult to buy guns by imposing rules such as long waiting times to purchase a gun, telling people where and when they can use guns, making it impossible to recognize concealed weapons laws from state to state, limiting the people who can buy them just because they may have had a hiccup sometime in their lives. During that last meeting with the NRA guy, Rellik, before the election, we also had this conversation.

Rellik: You know, Donald, it would be unfortunate if some President used Executive Orders to make law when it comes to Second Amendment rights. Don't you think so?

Me: That's just disrespectful of the Congress and its role in government. Believe me, if I'm elected, all laws will be enacted as our Founding Fathers envisioned: by Congress and not by one person who happens to be President. Of course, if my party has the majority in Congress, I will have the opportunity to do a little steering. Here it is: there will be no limits placed on the purchase of guns without laws passed by Congress. And if it goes the other way, I'll have a little thing called veto power. Oh, it might be all right for me to use Executive Orders to get what I want when it comes to guns; we'll make an exception when it comes to me using Executive Orders.

Rellik: Wait a minute. I think I have a check here for another $20-million.

I continued to support the NRA after I took office. I want those pistol-packing mammas and papas in the clutch. There will be another election and those guys and gals really turn out. I suppose it's a matter of wooing the fringe element, but a vote is a vote.

Topic 4: Womanizing

Okay, let's get on into it, maybe the real reason for this book, at least in the small minds of the religious fanatics and the stiffs. Yeah, I fooled around. At first, why not? I was single and apparently appealing to most women. And I was in a power position. Women always go for a guy who can give them a promotion or a raise. Even when they don't work for you, the very fact that you have this power position anywhere is a factor.

No one seemed to notice that I always hired the attractive ones.

Alice: I have a degree in English and an MBA. This job seems perfect for me.

Me: You're a very attractive woman. Nice smile. You know we deal with the public and I like to have people who are smart and make a good appearance.

Alice: Thank you. I know what you mean.

Me: And sometimes we have to travel together, so a bit of socialization is always possible.

From there, it was just a matter of where and when to make a move. It always surprised me that I never met very real resistance.

Alice: We shouldn't be doing this, should we?

Here are some of my favorite lines uttered by women at significant times:

Look, when someone comes on to you like I have, you need to come as long and as hard as you can.

Can we finish now?

We shouldn't be doing this, should we?

I can do a lot more if you want.

Do you like this? My husband loves it when I do that.

Wait! Let me think a minute ... okay.

Just wanted to see if I can make you hard.

I don't want to disappoint you.

Do anything you want.

Let me have a drag of this and then I don't care what you do.

Ta-da!

Oh, we're being naughty, aren't we?

I want you to teach me.

Can I see some I.D.? I want to be sure you're who you say you are.

I don't want to have sex. Do you want to just get naked and play around?

You've done this before, haven't you?

Ever do it in the shower? Let's take a shower.

Yeah, I'm not bashful about making moves. Sure, once in a while you run into a woman who's smarter than other broads, but that doesn't usually make a difference.

You know I'm a numbers guy, otherwise I couldn't be doing this wheeling and dealing that I do so well – I never really thought about it until I started writing this book – but I suppose I have had my share and more of sexual encounters. Let me see, about once a week since I was about twenty; that's 40 years. Hmm, that's over 2,000, isn't it?

Of course I'm counting those activities after 50 when I started hitting the strip bars and massage emporiums where a "happy ending" was a sure thing. The strip bars began to fascinate me after I tried a few. Of course, I went to some effort not to be recognized – changed my appearance a bit – but the guys at these places were highly unlikely to know me anyway. They weren't exactly Harvard graduates. The women in the strip bars were fascinating. How they get women to allow men to treat them that way is difficult for me to understand, but I'm not above taking advantage of it. And, of course, the more money you want to spend, the more you can take advantage.

Naturally, some of these encounters took place when I was single, but there were occurrences during marriages also. Yes I've been married. I think everyone knows of my beautiful current wife, Deborah, a former Victoria's Secret lingerie model. Let me tell you a bit about my four wives.

First there was Zina who managed to entrap me when I was 26. I thought I did pretty well staying a bachelor until that time, considering the women who were obviously making a play for me. Zina was a looker from Switzerland. I did some business with her father, and he was happy with the marriage. Unfortunately, she turned out to be a real shrew. She kept asking the wrong questions like "Where are you going?" or "Where have you been?" It was a nasty divorce, cost me a bundle.

Rachel was a wonder woman. She was a Yale graduate and was the CEO of a company she founded. You wouldn't believe the kind of company. No, it wasn't fashion design or real estate management or energy development. Instead, she did an extensive survey as part of her MBA thesis to determine what products or services were most needed. Office cleaning! In no time, she had thousands of clients and workers and a national company with franchisees using tools, costumes, and products that she developed. Occasionally, we ran into each other at airports. She never asked the Zina-type questions; she was too busy herself to care about my activities.

This may have been the ideal marriage except for one flaw: She cheated on me! At least I think she did. It all started when one of my friends saw her with a well-known jock at an opera of all places. I figure she talked him into going because she thought nobody I know would be there. It wasn't the opera I was concerned about; it was what happened after the opera. She gave me some BS about how she was lining him up to do a commercial. Yeah, right. You always get an opera-loving jock to endorse a cleaning service. And so that one went down the tubes.

My third marriage was to a woman who had deep, sensual eyes with a body that didn't stop. Paula Perpitrude I called her. She wasn't anywhere near as smart as my first two wives but she was a stunner. She was the maitre d' at one of the ritziest restaurants in the city. We hit it off immediately. I guess she knew a winner when she saw one, and I knew an amazing face and body when I saw one. Unfortunately, the luster wore off, especially when I saw what she looked like the first thing in the morning. God, it's incredible what women can do with their looks right out of a jar or tube.

I finally hit the jackpot with Deborah. She's everything I could possibly want. She knows all about my feelings about women and she understands. But now that I am where I am, there will be no more of that, even though we all know that there was more than one President who fooled around in the White House.

And there is more than one man who has used or is using his power to get what he wants from women. Some say that means disrespect. It depends on how you look at it. As long as we have two sexes, why not notice the difference, viva la difference. One of my oldest friends, Bill O'Liely, knew the difference.

Bill and I were buddies before I became President. Hell, we're still buddies. He came to all four of my stag parties. He would tell me about how he managed to get various women in bed. Sure, we laughed about it. What's not to laugh about?

O'Liely: I was at a convention of computer geeks. So many beautiful women standing in sales and information booths. When this one recognized who I was – the CEO of one of the largest tech firms in the country – it was like taking candy from a baby. Come to think of it, she was pretty much of a baby.

Me: You do those things right out there in the open?

O'Liely: People notice, but so what? There's certain lenience for those things for people like you and me, don't you think?

Me: Of course, but I'm not sure I want everyone talking about my successes along those lines. I try to keep those things hushed up.

O'Liely: I did, too, in the beginning, but now there are certain expectations. Look, I'm the CEO, but the guys who put me there are comrades in arms; they use women also.

Well, as everyone knows, Bill was fired after a half dozen of his female employees blew the whistle on him. I guess it took just one woman to start the avalanche and then the other women jumped in. Of course, the press was all over him. I stayed out of it pretty much. I had to respond to questions about Bill because everyone knew we were buddies. All I could say was the truth, that O'Liely was a good guy and that I didn't know anything about his personal escapades. Of course I knew about them; he bragged about them to me all the time. I just couldn't afford to have the public putting us in the same pothole.

Look, don't think that my life is all about sex. I'm multi-faceted.

Topic 5: Minorities

Have I ever had sex with a Black Woman? Sure. I have had sex with Caucasians, Blacks, Mexicans, but I'm interested mostly in White women in their 20s, 30, and 40s. I'm telling you this to prove that I don't discriminate, but I have my preferences.

I have minorities working for me throughout my companies, but I have to know that these employees are a whole lot smarter than the Whites in my employ. Take Tralicia:

Tralicia: Good morning. I used the couch in my office last night. I just had too many ideas running around in my brain. I was anxious to discuss some of them with you.

Me: Absolutely. I like the way you think.

That's what I like to see, but most of the Blacks do as little as they can. It's a strange combination – laziness and aggressiveness. That's the way I see it for the most part in Blacks; I guess I should say African Americans.

I like to keep some of them around so that no one can accuse me of racial discrimination, but I make sure that they're completely screened, but even with exercising greatest care, we still end up with some lazy and aggressive ones. What I don't understand is the lack of effort to step up in class. Right, I know we have had many who are credits to their race. I can see that. Then, take a look at television shows that feature Blacks. The music videos are disgraceful. All that jiggling around with obvious sexual innuendo is aimed at people – Black and White –

who have nothing more worthwhile on their minds. Even worse, I think, than the Blacks who are in the music videos are the Whites who act like them.

Look at all those NFL football players who kneel during the National Anthem. That's disgraceful. I think that the owners should fire their asses. I don't care why they say they do it. If they don't respect the American flag, they shouldn't be allowed to play professional football. If the college players kneel or sit during the National Anthem, they should lose their scholarships.

Another activity is how Blacks are featured in sit-coms. For a race that wants to progress, why do they appear in and watch actors with views and actions that are half a century old? With Whites, I know what I've got: people I can hire and fire based on performance. When I have to fire a Black, it's edgy. I hire them only if they're heads and shoulders above White applicants, but when I fire them, it's always with a concern that I'm going to be sued for racial discrimination.

Tralicia: I want to talk to you about the possibility of a promotion or a raise. I've been putting in an incredible number of hours and I think I've had extraordinary success in what I've accomplished.

Me: So?

Tralicia: Well, I've been in the same position for four years and – I don't want to say it – it seems to me that Caucasian woman around here are getting the promotions and the raises.

Me: Are you threatening me?

Tralicia: No, but I do think that there is not so subtle discrimination going on. I just want to be treated fairly.

Me: You said the magic word. You're fired. I have lawyers on the payroll that will take care of any suit you bring against me. I'll negotiate, I'll litigate, I'll settle, or I'll bribe. Whatever I have to do, I'll do. Sorry to see you go but, as I said, you're fired.

I don't have many of these situations, but when they happen, I know how to handle them. No Black and no woman can tell me what's fair and what's not fair.

While we're on the subject of minorities, let me give you my thoughts on Mexicans. Where do I start? They've invaded our country. They've brought with them drugs and violence. Yeah, yeah there are legitimate Mexican immigrants and there are Mexicans who have actually made contributions. I'll estimate one out of a hundred. The best thing we can do for our country is weed them out. I've never hired an illegal and I never will. If the illegal is Mexican, that policy is strictly in force.

We need to find a way to keep those illegals out of the U.S. Somebody suggested a wall between Mexico and the United States. That's not going to work. What we need to do is authorize border guards to shoot to kill. Kill enough of them and I think there's a real good possibility that the flow will slow.

I have a very workable policy on illegal immigrants who are already here. The cupcakes say that we can't break up families; we know that the kids born here are naturalized citizens. Nonsense. We need a law that says if the parent is illegal, so are the kids. Maybe there's already a law like that; I'll have to look into it.

I know it's not practical to locate and kick out every illegal. It seems to me that we have to deal with the problem of having them here, not just turn our heads. I think that we should start the process by prioritizing. They should get out of the country in this order:

1. Illegal immigrants convicted of a crime, any crime.
2. Illegal immigrants without families.
3. Illegal immigrants with families

If we never get to the third category, so be it.

Now the other category of minorities that concerns me is all of the Eastern Europeans trying to get into the United States because of conditions in their own countries. They come from Syria as well as other places that are unfriendly to our country. We know that many have hated us for years and now they want to find refuge here. Most of them are Muslims, a racial group or religious sect. Those are the last people we want here. They've chanted "Death to Americans" forever. How can you trust a group with that background? I understand we're a country open to "your tired, your poor," but let's not take in "your violent, your dangerous."

I'll be steering Congress into some action on limiting the number of refugees we allow in this country, and the small number that do get in will have to go through hell and back before they get any kind of free reign here. You know that even a traffic violation will get them kicked out. If any of them get a felony, we won't deport then, we'll lock them away with all the perverts we already have behind bars.

I know that many disagree with me on my refuge policies, my policy on not admitting them and my policy on getting rid of them if they are here illegally. Tough! I do what's best for the country instead of going overboard with the sympathy thing. What I want to do is Americanize America. Doesn't that sound reasonable?

Topic 6: Abortion

Sometimes, decisions have to be taken away from individual states. That's when the issue is very, very big, such as abortion. It just doesn't make any sense to have one state go one way on this and another state go another way. Abortion should be illegal across the board unless there are government-approved exceptions. That's why Roe v. Wade was an atrocious decision. Here's what happens because of that decision. A woman decides she wants a baby with blue eyes. The X-Rays tell her the baby's going to have brown eyes. It's within the first three months of the pregnancy. She has the baby killed. Does that sound legal or moral? I don't think so. We don't want pregnancies terminated because the baby is going to be a girl instead of a boy, because it appears that the baby has some small physical defect, or because the pregnant girl is not married.

It's about time that we say goodbye to Roe v. Wade. I'm going to do that by putting the right man on the Supreme Court bench. Yes, I said man. There are already too many women on the Court. We'll need a man to tilt the balance on this one. The Court has been stacked with way too many liberals. It's time for a big change. Of course, I've already discussed the seat with a number of hopefuls. Federal Judge Omar Priestly was one.

Me: Omar, you know that my primary concern with selecting the next Justice is to find someone who feels that abortion is an atrocity, someone who wants to see that infamous decision overturned.

Priestly: I know you feel that way, Mr. President, and it's a coincidence that I feel exactly the same way. If you were to select me for the Court, I can assure you that if I have the opportunity to be instrumental in assuring the end of abortion in our country, that's what I would do.

Then, I discussed the matter with another prospective appointee to the Court, Howard Priestly, who, coincidentally, is Omar's brother, both white men.

H. Priestly: As you know, Mr. President, I am a very religious man. I am guided not only by the Constitution in making my decisions but by the Bible. I find nothing in the Bible that can be interpreted as a right to take a life in the womb. Given the opportunity, I will tell you that my decisions would be guided by God as well as by man-made laws.

Me: I take it, then, that you are solidly against abortion and that you could be counted on to vote to overturn Roe v. Wade.

H. Priestly: Sir, you can depend on that.

Some potential Supreme Court Justices weren't so outspoken in their opinions about abortion. I interviewed several so-called conservative Federal Appellate Judges who gave me the old song about being totally objective until they have the opportunity to look at both sides of an issue. Clearly, they thought that's what I wanted to hear. Not a chance. I wanted a definite exclamation that the judge I appoint will help overturn Roe v. Wade.

Since I am telling all in this book, I will tell you that the issue of abortion has come into my personal life a few times. However, my thinking way back then was very different from my present thinking on this important issue.

The first time was in my early thirties. I was in my first marriage at the time. You remember Zina. The woman worked for me and we spent a great deal of time together on the job. The amazing thing is that I totally lucked out. She took it upon herself to get the abortion, never even told me about it. I remember she took some time off for one thing or another. I don't know because there were so many women in my life at the time. It wasn't until maybe a year later before another woman on the staff told me about it. Of course, she had no idea that I was responsible for the pregnancy. But then I thought, how do I know if I really was responsible? Who knows if she wasn't seeing other guys during that time? Frankly, though, it's a good bet that I was the one who planted the seed.

Then it happened again during the Paula marriage. This woman was ravishing. Sheila. We met at a charity fund-raiser. You know, I just didn't stop to use the necessary safeguards. I got reckless and it happened. This time, though, there was no doing the thing without my knowing about it. Instead, we discussed it. She needed money, of course, to make it happen and then to take some time off. We agreed that she should spend some time enjoying Paris. It cost me a bundle. It's odd how I thought more about the needs of the mother over the baby's. Well, that was a long time ago and I've changed.

One big reason I've changed, of course, is that being against abortion has been a solid plank in the Republican Party. I'm no fool. If I wanted to be the Republican candidate, I had to assume that position. There's no magic wand on this issue. I might as well be on the side of life when it comes to pregnancies. The best posture is to encourage adoptions, that kind of thing. Practically speaking, it's not going to make any difference at all what the law says. Women who want abortions will find a way to get them. There will always be doctors and others capable of doing the abortions outside of the law. I think we should outlaw abortions but not press too hard to enforce the law.

That brings us to the issue of Planned Parenthood. I suppose they do some good, such as counseling, handing out rubbers. Getting kids properly educated about the risks and the consequences is certainly a good thing. The problem is that Planned Parenthood has gone too far in enabling abortion. That's why it's time for at least a rap on the knuckles, maybe curtail their activities or at least take a hard look at what they're doing. And if Roe v. Wade gets overturned, we may have to put them out of business. I talked to the national director of Planned Parenthood, Cecelia Fortress, back before the election.

Me: Cece, I know that you guys do a lot of good, but I can't support this idea of anyone's right to an abortion under any circumstances. Should that be the case? What about that aborted baby who might become another Einstein or Martin Luther King?

Fortress: We believe strongly that every woman has a right to determine what can happen to her body. It's her body, for God's sake. Can government tell her to not get a tattoo, to order her how to cut her hair, to instruct her how to do her makeup? It's her body, hers.

Me: I understand. I respect women and women's rights, but this killing the baby thing, especially partial birth, is hard to accept.

Fortress: Would your opinion change if Planned Parenthood came up with maybe $20-million toward your campaign?

Me: If you could just take a harder look at those abortions that you support, maybe support abortions only if there is a very good reason for the abortion. I won't make any promises, but if you want to find that kind of money for the campaign, and ease up on the idea of abortions at will, I'll see what I can do if I become President.

Fortress: Would we still be able to sell body parts of aborted babies for research? I mean of course the money coming from that source would be only as much as we needed to provide the service.

Me: When could we get the $20-million?

Topic 7: LGBTQs

I know that most everyone who will read this book doesn't give a damn about this group of different people – LGBTQs. Many would not even know what those initials represent. Well, for the uninformed, L is for lesbian, women who enjoy doing it together, without men. G is for gay. It was hard for me to get used to that word to describe homosexuals. Hell, they're sad, not gay. I grew up thinking that word meant happy. B is for bisexual – going both ways, switch hitters we use to call them. T is for transvestite, guys who enjoy dressing up in women's clothing (ugh). Wait a minute! Maybe T is for transgender, someone who identifies with the other sex, maybe even had a sex change operation. And, finally, Q is for queer. That last is the word we used in my youth to refer to most of the above. Maybe Q is for something else and someone just added it to the LGBT as a joke. Who knows?

Actually, the whole thing sickens me, but we have been hit with a tsunami of understanding for everyone in this LGBTQ group over the past decade or so. It all comes from weeping hearts who feel, apparently, that even though they are not like you and me, they should have all the rights bestowed upon all Americans in the Constitution. It may surprise you that I am not totally devoid of understanding this feeling. I, too, believe that rights should not be dispensed selectively. Nevertheless, man, don't you think we have gone a bit around the bend on this? Do you want to stand beside everyone in that group or shouldn't we see if total freakishness hasn't provided the right for the rest of us to determine whether some rights shouldn't be withdrawn? Let's look at each of them in turn:

Lesbians. I don't have a problem with them. I don't understand them, but I don't have a problem with them. Personally, I understand some guys would not only approve but they would like to watch. The odd thing about them is that one of each couple of them apparently has to play the man. Hell, if that's the case, why don't they just go for the real thing? I remember Sally who used to be in my employ. Other staff members began to leak the lesbian information to me concerning Sally. Then I saw her one day huddled with her friend in a small bar. The other woman was wearing men's slacks, a dress shirt, and a hat that would look good on me. Her short haircut would have been a bit too short on most men. Being a great adventurer into the unknown, I ventured to raise the issue when we were alone.

Me: Saw you with a good-looking young guy a few days ago at Charlie's.

Sally: Young guy? No, I don't think you saw me. Charlie's?

Me: Yeah, the two of you looked, well, involved.

Sally: Oh, you're talking about my friend Elaine.

Me: Oh, Elaine. I guess she's a bit on the manly side.

Sally: I'm sorry, Mr. Thump, but I think you're getting into my personal life.

Why didn't she just say, "We're lovers and it's none of your business"? I guess she didn't say that because I'm the guy who can hand her walking papers. I delivered them anyway not long after that conversation. It occurred to me that her work was just shabby. Maybe if she had asked me to come and watch, she could have saved her job. What a waste. Anyway, I have no problem with Sally voting or having job protection; her work was just shabby. I have no intention of interfering with the rights of lesbians.

Gay. No problem as long as they don't get too close. I have had some gays working for me, no doubt. We all know that they have artistic talents, and that can be very useful in some jobs. Sure, you get a little nauseous when they walk and talk, but I guess they're not all that way. One of my friends told me about a conversation he had with a gay guy.

My friend: You know, Steven, it's none of my business, but I think everybody knows you're gay. You are openly gay, aren't you?

Steven: Yes, I am. Are you straight?

My friend: Yes but that doesn't mean that I don't understand gays and their needs.

Steven: You have no idea about my needs. I have a voracious appetite for sex with other gay men. I'll probably never see you again because I'm going back to San Francisco. I was there for seven years. I'm guessing that I had sex maybe a thousand times during those seven years. Impressive, huh?

My friend: Ah, yea, if you say so.

So, why not all rights for gays also even if that makes straight males uncomfortable?

Bisexuals. Well, this goes beyond my understanding. They like both guys and gals and will do it with either or both at the same time for all I know. Again, it's pathetic but let them vote, have equal rights in the workplace, etc.

Transgenders. This has caused more ruckus than any of the others combined. I guess it's because you can be a lesbian, gay, or bi-sexual and we can do end runs on all of those folks. They don't interfere with our rights of privacy. Now, the transgender men want to go into the ladies' restroom and vice versa. Everyone's up in arms about these guys who see themselves as women cruising into a ladies' room occupied by some young women. North

Carolina got so excited about it that they passed a law preventing them from that visitation. Then the liberals went crazy, pulled all kinds of business out of the state. I asked a North Carolina Senator about what the discussion was like when that bill was being considered.

Me: This is a very courageous bill, considering the general feeling of the country now toward LGBTQs.

Senator Ram: It's the Ts we have a problem with. How can we let a little girl go into a restroom, a ladies' restroom, when there may be some pervert in there?

Me: Yea, I see your concern. But what if that pervert – I mean man – really believes he's female?

Senator Ram: We're not taking any chances. Besides, even if he thinks he's a she, he probably still looks like a hairy man. That's going to scare the hell out of that little girl.

Me: I couldn't agree with you more, but do you have enough votes and a governor that will hang tough?

Senator Ram: We'll go to the U.S. Supreme Court if we have to. Of course, we'll need a right-thinking President to appoint a right-thinking Justice to the Court.

Apparently, there are many, many members of this LGBTQ group, so my opinion is to let it slide. After all, they're all voters.

Topic 8: The Disabled

Sure, they need help because they can't do what everyone else can do, but why is everyone else on the hook to provide that help – businesses that have to provide handicap parking space and handicap working conditions? And, of course, employers are required to hire or promote someone in direct competition with those who are not disabled. It seems to be that the disabled got a bad break. Why does everyone else have to suffer? I remember a guy who had no sympathy for the disabled. Since he was in good shape, he told jokes about disabled people.

Karl Sludge: Hear about the guy who lost his index finger, his ring finger, and his pinkie in an industrial accident? Every time he waved at somebody, they thought he was giving them the finger.

Me: Ouch. I bet he got punched out a lot.

Karl: Then there was the guy who had gangrene in one leg but the doctors cut off the wrong leg. He sued the doctors but the case was thrown out. The judge said the guy didn't have a leg to stand on.

Me: How about this? Police arrested a thalidomide couple at the airport. They were charged with trying to take small arms aboard a plane.

So you think I'm insensitive. Here's the point. Most of these people are up to working right along with the rest of us. There are documented cases of disabled individuals holding their own. How about Helen Keller? What happens is they become specially privileged people, taking in government funds, getting jobs that more qualified people might get, having the closest parking spaces when they often don't really need them.

Am I going to get in the way of their privileges? Of course not. They vote, don't they?

Topic 9: Bullying

I didn't take any guff from anybody when I was a kid. At ten years old, I was a pretty strong little monster. I used to walk up to groups of other kids and say, "I can beat up anybody here," No one ever challenged me. A few times, a kid got in my way and I had to beat up on him. I only did what was necessary. Once, when I was a teenager, a guy pushed one of my friends. This guy was tall and thin, about 17. I was 16 at the time. One punch to the midsection from me and it was all over. I've always protected my friends, did it when I was a kid, still do it.

I remember running into a kid I didn't particularly like when we were both crossing a vacant lot. When I stopped him and asked him what he was doing there, he got real nervous, so I thought I would have a little fun with him.

Me: You're the kid who's been talking about me at school.

Francis Broadhead: Me? No, I haven't been talking about you.

I could see he was shaking in his boots.

Me: No, you're the one. I'm sure you're the one.

Francis: I have to go. My brother will be looking for me.

Me: Is your brother a broad head, too?

Francis: That's just my name.

Me: I can beat up you and your brother with one hand tied behind my back.

Now the kid is probably leaking in his pants.

Francis: I have to go.

Me: Don't let me see you around here again. You got that?

Pretty much, I always got what I wanted when I was a kid. Why not? My family had a lot more cash than the other kids. And I'm a good-looking guy as I've been told by many of the opposite sex. When I threw a party, I picked out the kids I wanted in attendance. When I invited them, they came. I figure if you have money, looks, and muscle, you have it all, so why not cash in those chips. Of course, I've mellowed since I've been an adult, but I still don't mind throwing around a little of those assets when necessary.

You have to bring up your sons to be tough also. That's part of being a good father. I admired one father in my neighborhood. His son came home with a bloody nose after being in a fight. What did his father do? Did he feel sorry for him or pamper him? Nope. What he did was send his son back out, right then and there, and told him not to come home until he gave that other kid a bloody nose.

I've always felt that you had to have the power and you had to display it. That's one reason why I will have a great record as President when it comes to foreign affairs. We're not going to back down to any nation. I had many friends when I was a kid, not because I was nice to them or because I paid the bill at the candy shop, but because they were afraid of me. It works that way for nations, too. If they fear us, they will be our friends.

From what I've told you, you probably think I was a bully when I was a kid. Maybe you're right, but I'll tell you something that will surprise you. Let me illustrate by telling you about the time I didn't like the umpire's calls during a baseball game I was pitching when I was about 16, so I accused him of favoring the other team because he had friends on that team. The second baseman of the other team, Terry, walks over and around me just looking for trouble. I hit him hard. He came back but I really put it to him before everybody jumped in to break us up. I ran into him a few weeks later.

Me: Hey, Terry, how you doing Buddy.

Terry: I'm okay. The side of my jaw is still a little sore.

Me: Sorry, guy. I got in a few good punches. How about you come over this weekend? I'm having some friends in I want you to meet. We'll have a good time. We're friends now, right?

Terry: Well, sure, I guess.

Me: Come on over, we'll play some ball and I'm buying the dogs.

See what I mean? Maybe I had a little bully in me, but anybody who stood up to me became my friend.

Topic 10: Health Insurance

What a mess! I could have called this book How I Got to Be President. A former President's attempt to bring affordable care to millions is one big reason how I got to be President. Members of my party hated that law from the get-go. Why? Because it made sense. It worked. It did allow many who were uninsured to obtain economical protection against long or sudden stays in a hospital, treatment in urgent care centers, and doctor bills. The law allowed people to get proper medical care, not quick brush-off charity from doctors and hospitals. My party hated it because it was the other party that put it together.

What intrigued me from the beginning was that my party, the Republicans, successfully convinced themselves it was a bad law, primarily because the former non-insured were forced to buy the insurance or pay a penalty. This small hiccup became a booming explosion. Republicans convinced themselves and then convinced everybody else, everyone but those folks who now had insurance protection at a reasonable cost. My opponent in the general election vowed to support and expand that law. Bingo! Since we convinced so many voters that the Democrats were the big, bad guys on this – even though I knew they were the good guys – I rode it hard to a win in November. It was Nazi propaganda at its best, telling a lie so many times that it was believed by all, even though it was an obvious lie. Oh, it's not the only reason I won, of course, but it sure helped.

I talked to an insurance CEO about the former President's plan to provide affordable medical care.

John Defonious: Let me tell you about this idea, Donald. It's a hell of an idea. You see, it brings customers to our industry. That's the best thing about it. Now we have 20-million people who have to buy insurance, customers knocking at our doors.

Me: But these may not be the customers you want, John. You can't turn down people who have diabetes, heart disease, and other kinds of ugly problems.

Defonious: Bring 'em in. We can set the premiums to cover those folks with necessary increases over the years, despite the President's talk about keeping the rates low. We have to find a way to make a profit out of all this; we're not not-for-profits in the insurance industry.

Get it? Twenty million people are happy because they have insurance coverage, the hospitals and doctors are happy because they're going to get paid, and the insurance companies are happy because profits increase. Why our party hates the law so much is beyond me, except for one important factor: We've convinced the majority of the voters that somehow it's a bad law. Therefore, we took advantage of that fact and harped on it throughout the campaign.

Now I'm in a position to dump the law or create one in my own image, but it's not going to be easy – and it may take most of my administration to make the necessary changes. Probably the best thing I can do is ponder it and investigate it and committee it for four years and then blow it away along with all the formerly uninsured. I need to rivet my attention on more important matters.

I will say in passing that if I'm so inclined I could put together a law that would be far superior to the existing law. It would require cutting certain expenses drastically. I'm talking Medicare and Medicaid. Medicaid's easy. Get rid of the free-loaders. There has to be millions of them. I'd replace the bleeding hearts with some tough decision makers to determine who's qualified for Medicaid. Medicare would be a little tougher with AARP resistance and the fact that senior citizens vote. It would require the help of the medical profession. Doctors have to find a way of reducing costs – use better methods, materials, younger doctors, whatever.

I have a friend who wrote a novel with a perfect solution, but we may not be ready yet for this. In the novel, the government took care of everyone's health care, but if anyone contracted a problem that would be expensive to treat, that person was removed permanently. Imagine how much money that would save.

Topic 11: Social Security

I thought about privatization of Social Security long before anyone used the term. Way back when I was about 23, a neighbor told me about how he had worked 45 years on a job and was living mostly on this government check every month. When I thought about how much money was taken out of his paycheck compared to what he was getting and because I already knew about the future value of money, I came to the conclusion that he was being royally screwed over.

It doesn't take a rocket science to realize that the government isn't the best investment for a long-time worker. Why not give everyone the option of determining how those funds should be invested? I had the opportunity to ask a U.S. Senator about that around that time when he was a speaker at a convention I attended.

Me: Senator, has Congress ever considered allowing workers to invest the funds privately instead of putting them into the Social Security fund?

Senator Mudgraft: No, we never considered that. Next question.

I doubt that he even understood my point. Look at what's happening. Money is automatically taken out of paychecks and handed over to the government. What does the government do with it? It's handed out to individuals at a rate of return that's pathetic, then it goes to those who never really earned it: the disabled, survivors, and thieves. The system needs total revamping, something that prior administrations were frightened silly to do.

I'll be appointing a group of financial advisers to give Social Security a hard look to move toward a restructured system. It's not going to be easy with seniors now collecting Social Security checks. I suppose they'll have to be grandfathered (and grandmothered) in. Obviously, the original plan didn't take into consideration that some of the folks would live so long. That little problem always reminds me of Johnny Sharpie. You couldn't talk about old folks around him because everything was a joke.

Johnny: What do they do with Volkswagen Beetles when they don't run anymore?

Me: What do they do with them?

Johnnie: They put them in old Volks homes. Ha, ha, ha.

That's why Johnnie won't be a member of my investigation and planning group on Social Security. The trouble is that Social Security is a joke. It doesn't work. The fund is running out of money. If we don't make a change pronto, we'll have to find new sources of money to support the program. I'm not waiting around for the fund to go dry, especially not on my watch.

Look, I have become very, very rich because I know where to put my money. I want the American people to have that same opportunity. They'll never do it as well as I have, of course, but they will have an excellent chance if they receive proper guidance from my administration, not let their money go into a deteriorating government fund. As everyone knows, I am very smart when it comes to money. That's my advice and I'm going to start the engines on this one: get rid of social security over the long haul and make people a whole lot wealthier by doing so.

So, what do we do about those who are permanently fixed to the system, people now collecting social security? First we change eligibility for collecting checks to 75. Too many people are working way after 65 and living into their nineties. As for the disabled and survivors, we need to decrease the amount they receive. They're being overpaid. These moves will save the fund while we change the way the system works.

Topic 12: Tax Records

The Democrats did their best to make the availability or non-availability of my tax records a political issue. Is it anybody's damn business how much money I make? Is it my fault that no past candidate ever had as much money? Do I need everyone looking into my financial bedroom window? Maybe the supposed issue is whether I paid any taxes from all the money I've made, but I think the real issue is how much money I've been able to amass over the years. That's really what the Democrats want to reveal. They think that if all that is laid out, the public will find illegality, dishonesty, avarice, and cruelty, and guess what? If I revealed all of my tax records, the public would find illegality, dishonesty, avarice, and cruelty. How in the hell can you make the fortune I've made without those steps along the way? Sure, I can simply say that I've hired good lawyers to find tax loopholes and that, in fact, I haven't paid any taxes - none. Bernie Schultzpace has been my primary tax advisor for a long time.

Me: Bernie, I'm going to take in an enormous amount of money in real estate deals this year. What can we do to minimize taxes?

Schultzpace: Minimize them? You're talking to the wrong lawyer if you want to minimize them. How about no taxes? We'll find a way.

Me: Can we do that legally?

Schultzpace: Yeah, yeah. There are tax-free exchanges, and there's charitable giving, even if it's mysteriously done through multiple loopholes. Don't sweat it. We'll make it happen.

Me: Bernie, you will have my full cooperation in this endeavor.

I listed above some of what the public would have discovered about me if I had released all of my tax records. I'll be more specific.

Illegality. If you think that Bernie Schutlzpace was on the up and up when he advised me about taxes, you are certainly mistaken. I didn't pay him the big bucks because he could read the tax code. We didn't avoid taxes, we evaded taxes. Anyway we could. That sometimes required a second or third set of books. It sometimes meant setting up tax shelters. Sometimes, it meant the money was earned in dealings with the underworld. Yes, unlike Richard Nixon who professed not to be a crook, I am a crook.

Dishonesty. A careful scrutiny of released tax records would probably result in the conclusion that I lied about certain financial matters. I'm not George Washington who never told a lie or Honest Abe. I'm Donald Thump and I learned early on how to lie and that lying paid.

Big investor Joe McFortune: Donald, do we have the facts pertaining to this merger?

Me: Absolutely. We had our books audited by one of the top accounting firms in the country.

Yeah, right.

McFortune: I know the books are complete and accurate. I take it that there are no possible lawsuits down the road and that the products have a great future.

Me: This merger means our stock is going to go through the roof. I'm getting you in on the ground floor.

The products were cheap and dangerous; I saw some products liability possibilities in the near future but by that time we had bailed out, leaving the investors up the creek without the proverbial paddle.

Avarice. The careful purveyor of my tax records would notice that we swallowed up real estate at a prestigious rate. Schultzpace always found a way to effect tax-free exchanges. I couldn't get enough. I was particularly enamored with quality commercial real estate - places with golf courses, tennis courts, and swimming pools. I never shied away from flaunting it when I happened upon one of the many who paid through the teeth to live in one of my places. Jack Stone lived in one of my condos.

Jack: Man, this is living. I don't know how long I can stay here before my cash runs out, but I'm enjoying it as long as I can.

Me: I take it you enjoy the golf course, the pool, and the beautiful woman that we manage to have available.

Jack: You got it. I don't know how you do it, but I'm not asking. Just keep up the good work.

Cruelty. I've never had any pity for the suckers. This is America. We all have equal opportunity, so when I see a homeless person, a bum asking for change, or a disabled person working the system, I figure they're getting what they deserve: a loser mentality. Why should I waste my time feeling sorry for these people? And I don't concern myself with losers who are not in those categories, guys who don't have the guts to do what's necessary to get ahead. Ben Cringemore was one of those.

Me: Ben, you're not cutting it. You've had opportunities to make this company work and you've failed. I'm cutting the string.

Ben: You mean I'm out? I've devoted 20 years to making this company go. You can't just take the company over and send me on my way.

Me: That's exactly what I'm going to do. You're gone.

Ben: Please don't do that, Donald. I have three kids in high school. I have college expenses ahead. And you know that my wife has been ill for a year now. I can't afford the insurance if I don't have this job.

Me: None of that concerns me. You're out.

Ben: Will I get some kind of helpful recommendation from you? I'll need to get another position as soon as possible.

Me: Naw, you should have thought of that years ago. Clean out your desk. Security is going to see you out.

You can call it cruelty; I call it good business. Maybe those personal interactions won't show up in tax records, but some assumptions along those lines might be ascertained.

I couldn't let the public gather in any of that information during the Presidential campaign. Obviously, it would not have helped my cause. More importantly, I couldn't let the public know that I paid zero taxes. You know how many voters would have gotten all caught up in how I should be paying my part to support the country. Let the suckers support the country. I believe in the old adage of charity beginning at home. I also believe that charity begins and ends at home. What's truly amazing is that if the voters knew about my practices, many would admire me for them and the votes would still come tumbling in.

Topic 13: Election Fraud

I still find it hard to believe that my opponent ended up with 3-million more votes. The Electoral College got it right, of course, but it still frosts my buns that my opponent supposedly received all those additional popular votes. There had to be some fraud involved, but how did the Democrats do it is the question. I have some theories.

1. Too many of the voting booths have junk equipment. The right guy in a precinct can find a way to make some subtle, unnoticed changes that would award more votes than deserved for one of the candidates. I can't say how it's done, but it is obvious that some of the counting is rotten.

2. Reporting the votes is a human factor. This is where the opportunists come in, if the Democrats at a specific precinct can outflank the other watchers of the polls.

3. Collusion. This is where the Republican watchers go over to the other side. Traitors.

The combination of those ingredients cooked up some horrible soup. Please tell me how I could have scored so well in state after state while votes were being piled up for my opponent. It just doesn't make sense. It is my thinking that there were many voters – even though they were in the minority, I think, when it came elections time – who envied me and knew that I was going to shake up their world. It's clear that many of these were members of the so-called intelligencia, people with college and master's degrees. They were in positions to influence the election though fraudulent behavior. So, some of it was lousy equipment and insufficient safeguards, but primarily we are looking at plain old cheating on the part of people who were in the position to cheat.

I guess I shouldn't resent having the popular vote taken away from me when I won the one that mattered – the electoral vote – but it's still embarrassing and disappointing. I won the big one, and that's all that's important. There's talk about changing the system so that Presidents are elected by popular vote. It's not going to happen on my watch. The Electoral College prevents only the big states from deciding who's going to be President. Representation from all the states is necessary.

I won because I was smart enough to know where to put the money and where to be during the campaign. My opponent wasn't in the right place at the right time. End of story and end of opponent.

Topic 14: My Cabinet Choices

Houdini couldn't have done it better. My slight-of-hand choices for the cabinet were magical. Democrats couldn't believe what was happening. They watched hopelessly as I announced one selection after another. The biggest laugh was how I paraded enemies, Republicans who didn't support me as well as Democrats before the world as possible selections. Yeah, that's going to happen. Some of them actually believed that they had a chance. I always thought that I could have been a great actor. My strategy was to have the public think that I was going to a appoint some favorite of the public to a post and then quickly announce my real choice, followed by pushing the appointee through the Senate with lightning speed.

The truth is that I didn't have a clue what most of these departments did, so I had to do a little crash reading. I might still be a little hazy, but I appointed people who seem to be right for the job. I'll talk about some of them.

Secretary of State. I knew, of course, that this was an important one. It's the person who represents us throughout the world, the person who puts out the fires and brings nations together. At least that's what I understand Henry Kissinger did. My idea was to appoint a man of Kissinger's caliber without the accent. I really pondered this one but came up with Dennis Traveler. I figured that his last name was really close to travel so he was perfectly suited for the job.

Secretary of Agriculture. Well, we have to feed the country. Although I'm not personally interested in stepping in the dung of cattle or sitting behind the wheel of a tractor, I admire those who can do it and do it right. For Secretary of Agriculture, I had to find someone who knew what farmers did and how they did it. For this job, I found Henry Carroton because someone told me that he once ran a fruit stand for his family before he went to college and actually studied agriculture.

Chairman of the Joint Chiefs of Staff. I knew I would be seeing a whole lot of this person in the White House so I slipped in a former model who became a millionaire by inventing a restructured bra. I figured that she was a well-organized individual and it would be fun to have her around.

Secretary of Energy. Ben Windsor, I thought, was the man for the job. He has a thorough understanding of energy because he owned a hundred or so windmills a few years ago. He also has a good friend who owns an oil business and he knows some of my golf friends who are also into oil. I like the idea of nuclear power also. We need to have power and backups to power. You know how annoying it is when you lose your TV signal right in the middle of a reality show.

Secretary of HUD. This appointment hasn't been made yet. I'm still trying to figure out exactly what they do. I think Hud was a Paul Newman movie once, but I don't think there's a connection there.

Secretary of Treasury. This one I understand because it involves money, something I know. I had a dozen good choices for this job, people who helped me in financial dealings over the years. I finally decided on Greg Moneybags, a man who is almost as rich as I am (although, frankly, not as smart). If we run into a shortage of money, I'm sure Greg will know enough to print some more.

Secretary of Commerce. We want trade between and among the states to flourish. I'm concerned, however, with the trade agreements in place with foreign countries, especially China. Marcel Foghorn has been the French Ambassador and once ran a company that traded in antique items. He has a certain feel for how the economy should flow.

Me: I'm interested in international commerce that allows us to produce goods that are sold at a definite advantage to the United States.

Foghorn: Exactly. We need to get China and other Asian nations, as well as some European nations, to buy our products at ridiculously high prices while we continue to purchase their goods at bargain prices.

Me: How do we do that?

Foghorn: Rip up all trade agreements so we can start from scratch and then impose our will on these less economically successful countries.

Me: I like the way you think. You're my man.

Secretary of Homeland Security. This one, of course, is of primary concern. We know that refugees pose a great danger to the country. We know we have to end that threat by accepting very few refugees each year, maybe keep it to a dozen or so. Then we have to vastly increase police power. I'm looking at a plan whereby we quadruple our police forces. This might mean that we loosen up the tight hiring requirements. I think that the tests now administered keep too many potentially excellent officers from ever serving. Those personality tests, for example showing that applicants are prone to bullying, should be abolished. We need people who can exert their wills to get the best results. Intimidation works; I've used that approach for years.

Me: How can we best protect our country?

Melvin Strongforce: I think we should implement a police state without anyone noticing that it's a police state. Sure, we can still want all the good things police officers do – help stranded motorists, give directions – but we have to err on the side of safety. We need to pay special attention to anyone with an accent or anyone who dresses differently. To be safe, we have to be diligent.

Me: I think that we're on the same page. I'm appointing you to Homeland Security.

Secretary of Interior. I interviewed Justin Timberriver about Interior.

Me: I understand that you camp out a lot.

Timberriver: Yes, well not in tents or things like that. My wife and I do enjoy taking a weekend once in a while and spending it at a rural Holiday Inn.

Me: Oh, good. You've been to Yellowstone, I take it.

Timberriver: Yes, we loved going there, been there twice in fact. We loved it so much that we call our brownstone Yellowstone.

Me: And the forests and woods. You want those preserved, right?

Timberriver: Is it true that if a gun goes off in the woods and there is no one there it will make no sound?

Secretary of Education: Edwin Noghead was my immediate choice. He believes as I do that there is too much money spent on public education.

Noghead: The problem is that we spend all those dollars to educate only a few.

Me: I don't understand. We're educating millions in public schools.

Noghead: Not really, sir. You see only about 20% of the students have any interest in learning. Many are there because the law says they have to be there. In response, they have absolutely

49

no interest in learning. They can't wait until they reach 16 so they can leave. Then there are those who treat high school as a mating ritual. And, of course, you have all those black kids who want to be professional athletes so they stay around but really don't pay much attention to teachers.

Me: Don't we have white kids too who want to be pros?

Noghead: Sure, but their families will push them eventually into some serious career path.

Me: What do we do about the high cost of public education?

Noghead: Private schools. Let the serious kids go to private schools. Since the other kids aren't interested in learning anyway, we'll let the public schools deteriorate, we'll combine schools, and we'll discourage students from completing high school and steer them into other hourly pay situations. Fast food restaurants are constantly looking for good, cheap help. Yes, we need to facilitate good students getting into charter, magnet, religious, and other alternative schools in order to improve the education of kids and to save government money.

Me: You sound like you've got a handle on this. Just as long as we cut costs for public education that is not wanted or appreciated.

Secretary of Labor: I didn't labor over this one. A little joke there. I don't exactly have a romance with labor. I've had to avoid the outrageous demands of labor all my adult life. Unions are outdated and need to be removed as a force in industry. Maybe years ago when kids were put to work or people were forced to work under dangerous conditions, unions served a purpose. The time for any need for unions has long passed. Companies are interested in producing good products at the lowest possible cost. Unions just get in the way. I searched for a Labor Secretary who would minimize the impact of unions while working with large corporations as well as small companies to assure fair treatment of workers. Buddy Strongarm is an old friend who will be perfect for this job. He managed to CEO several major companies that were always able to fight union efforts. How did he do it? He always managed to get it across to his employees that they would be out on the street if they voted in a union. He was subtle but effective in accomplishing that. He's my man for Secretary of Labor.

Secretary of Veteran's Affairs. I know a guy who was drafted during the Korean Conflict. He sat behind a desk and shuffled papers in a safe building in Germany. Sometime during that two-year period he developed flat feet by working out in a gym provided to him. He still collects money from the VA for his war injuries. Come on! He had his college paid for him by the government because of his service. From the time he was discharged, he received inexpensive medical care and prescriptions from the VA. All for two years behind a desk and flat feet. The question is how long should the VA be responsible for minor or unconnected injuries? I'm having my good friend Arnold Gibanger take a hard look at this. Of course, I also want him to make sure that the real wounded get proper treatment and that the VA hospitals shape up. That's where we'll put the money that's wasted on the veterans who don't really deserve costly care or checks in the mail.

Director of the Environmental Protection Agency. I knew that Fazio Allover would be perfect for this job.

Me: Everyone seems to be concerned about the climate. What's your take on that?

Allover: Ever since that damn Gore movie, it seems that there is some concern about the climate. Sure it's warmer now. That's good, isn't it?

Me: I need someone in this job who will protect the environment. Do you think that the environment needs protection?

Allover: There may be some evidence of climate change, and it's possible that there could be human involvement in this change.

Me: But not enough to concern us?

Allover: We can conjure up some laws to lessen carbon emission maybe. However, I wouldn't get too excited about it.

Me: Okay, I guess you know what you're talking about.

My nominees flew through confirmation, of course. We had more Republicans than Democrats on the Senate committees and we had more Republicans than Democrats in the Senate. Oh, sure, a few Republicans made some noises about my choices, like how they were going to ask tough questions, but in the end, they voted with the party. All of my nominees were confirmed.

Topic 15: My Wife and Children

Zina, my first wife, bore my first child, Dunkin. Rachel was the mother of my second child, Mellow. Dunkin, of course, is my son and Mellow is my very bright daughter. They have worked with me in one or another of my companies for the last 15 years or so. I expect that both of them will be very helpful in my administration just as my present wife, Deborah, will be. I am considering important posts for all of them. After all, John F. Kennedy appointed his brother Robert Attorney General so there's some precedent for having family members involved in running the country.

Dunkin is my Chief of Staff for the time being. He had a minor in Government in college although his major was Business Administration, of course. He brings to the job a very logical mind with enormous organizational skills. He'll help us stay pointed in the right direction on a day-to-day basis. Long-term, after the country has acclimated to having him in this position, I am considering a step up for him by his replacing one of the flunkies I've appointed to Cabinet jobs. Maybe Labor.

Mellow is a Presidential Assistant as this point. I'm going to steer her toward Commerce, I think. She was a Marketing major.

Deborah may be satisfied to be a first lady for a while. I'm sure that she will be involved in matters that will have impact on women all over the country. Her choice of clothes, of course, even outer garments, is spectacular. She will probably continue to model for charity events. Once she takes real interest on how government works, I wouldn't be surprised if she begins to think of a more important role. She mentioned that Robin Wright became Ambassador to the United Nations in House of Cards, a TV series. She might be looking in that direction.

Some people might think that I'm going too far by considering my wife and kids for some lofty positions, but let me tell you that they are very smart and can do whatever they want. We could be making that move immediately; just stay tuned.

Topic 16: Hollywood

Because of my respect for Ronald Reagan and Charlton Heston, I find it difficult to criticize anyone in Fluffland, but the way I've been treated by most of those Hollywood "stars" has been abominable. It all started during the campaign, of course, when there was immense publicity about big stars going door to door in behalf of my opponent. How they can believe that they have any real understanding of government and politics is beyond me. But that didn't stop Merle Steep, Jane Honda, Reese Winterspoon, Sally Stream, Clint Westwood, Robert Greenford, and Brad Litt from attacking my qualifications. As far as I'm concerned, they're all no-talents, but let's examine what each of them had to say and why they were totally incorrect in their statements.

Steep. She said I didn't respect the disabled. I've explained my position on the disabled. It's not that I don't respect them; it's just that we give them way more than they deserve. Hell, I respect disabled individuals if only they get past their bad luck and do something other than get in the way of the rest of us who don't need their whining. So she's won a couple of Oscars. Those were bad years for the movies, not many good performances.

Honda. She comes from a family that feels it has special privileges in Hollywood, entitling her to speak out against government intervention in foreign lands. She wouldn't even be in the movies if her father and brother didn't pave the way for her, giving her a free pass. People didn't listen to her the first time so why should they listen to her when she says I'm not morally fit to be President? How can anyone in Hollywood talk about moral fitness? They party all the time, trade partners, and perform in indecent movies. She's a leader of the morally unfit.

Reese Winterspoon. She said that my opponent was going to win so big that it might be the beginning of the end for the Republican Party, another stupid opinion from a stupid person. She was a child star because her mother slept with a director. From there, she learned how to act (with directors as well as in the movies). She didn't even know my opponent, and she certainly doesn't know me. That doesn't stop her from continuing her Hollywood attacks on the President of the United States. Put her in a bundle with the rest.

Sally Stream. Another golden oldie. She started on television playing a nun. Maybe that's why she's full of that holier-than-thou crap. She said that no man who has never held an elective position is qualified to be President. What does she know? I say no so-so actress who has never gone to acting school is qualified to be in the movies. Obviously, she doesn't have a clue as to my credentials. It appears to me that she just wants to be a member of the Hollywood crowd that despises me because their candidate didn't win. She wants to be liked.

Clint Westwood. I can understand the actresses, I suppose. After all, their candidate was a woman. They couldn't understand that she was an unqualified woman. Now, this guy peeps in. He used to ride a horse in movies. I think he took one too many gallops. Now, he's a director. It's odd how movie directors think they can direct the world. It's fantasy, Clint. That's all. He told the press that I would never make it as President, that he expected me to be impeached maybe even before I took office. I can't tell you what he was talking about because he didn't know what he was talking about. Get a life, Clint.

Robert Greenford. Here's a winner finally, a guy who can act. So I won't disparage his art. I'll just tell you that he doesn't have a clue when he steps out of his comfort zone. He played a baseball player once and did all right with that part. I enjoyed the movie. Then last spring he has his film festival and announces that we will not support me because I was not qualified to be President. People went to his film festival to see movies, not hear his opinion about matters beyond his comprehension. Nevertheless, he said that I wasn't qualified to be the President's butler much less the President. Here's another guy who should just stick to what he knows. I'll get my revenge with him. I'll find plenty wrong with his next movie and I'll be in the position to sink it. I hope it's about a ship.

Brad Litt. He made a movie once about two women going on a wild spree. His character makes out with one of the women and then steals all their money. That's pretty much what he's done in real life. Real life imitates art. Ever since that movie, he's stolen two other men's wives. How can anyone who can't be trusted with your wife have time to know anything about government? He says that I'm a woman hater and a sexist. That's the pot calling the kettle black. I don't think that he should express opinions about me when he's no better than I am.

Anyway, who cares about these Hollywood peep squeaks? I could buy out all their studios and leave them in the unemployment line. I'm going to consider doing just that as soon as I have the time to deal with Hollywood. I'm kind of busy right now.

Topic 17: I Won!!!

I will tell you that I had the shock of my life election night. I was sitting in my living room with Deborah at my feet working on my concession speech. It was going to be glorious, how I fought the good fight, how I worked hard for the party, and how I admired my opponent for putting it all together for the victory. I wasn't going to mention that I knew I was going to lose from the start. How could I possibly win? She had everything: experience, likeability, the party solidly behind her, millions of contributors. What did I have? Well, a desire to have a great time running for the Presidency of the United States. So I played it for kicks. As long as I was going in for the laughs, I thought I would insult practically every person, group, and entity in the country. I thought I might as well also throw in my disdain for the U.S. Constitution.

Little did I know that a strategy anywhere near that one would result in a victory. What the hell!! To my amazement, my approach resulted in enough electoral votes to win the Presidency. People actually liked my ranting and raving. Here's some of what I said during the campaign that roused mostly white middle class folks.

Shoot to kill. I was very vocal about protecting our Mexican border. There was astonishment that I would say such a thing, but all those nervous residents of Texas, Arizona, and California especially loved what I had to say. They believed that the only way to keep out illegal Mexicans is to send a very big message: cross the border and you may die. I heightened the fear and apprehension by pointing out accurately that many drugs were coming into the country through an insecure border and that many of these illegal immigrants were responsible for vicious crimes in the United States.

Loosen gun controls. The Second Amendment lovers have a thing going with their guns. They're proud owners and probably take them to bed with them. They're not satisfied with one-shot-at-a-time pieces either. They want the latest technology, rapid-fire rifles and pistols. And they don't want anyone interfering with how quickly they can obtain these guns, no nonsense about having to wait to get them. If they want them, they want them now. We all know that the Second Amendment right to arms was to protect the people from a government gone wrong. We also know that the kinds of guns we have now weren't even envisioned back in the late 1700s. Nevertheless, these would-be cowboys point to the Constitution as a right to buy any kind of gun anytime.

Now, I'm not really crazy about everyone packing all around me with weapons that can shred a body in seconds, but there are many, many gun-crazy voters out there so this was an easy one to embrace. Add the fact that there is this far-out organization, the National Rifle Association, that seems to have its way with politicians, and I was the recipient of an incredible amount of votes and money. It's hard for me to believe this organization is for real, but why look a gift horse in the mouth?

Women. This tactic was carefully calculated. I knew that a lot of men would get a real kick out of my insulting women, especially pedantic women. More men would enjoy the news that I treated women in general with very little respect. At the same time, I knew that I wouldn't lose the entire women vote because there are enough ignorant women out there who would still vote for me. My insulting of some women was done boldly and openly on TV and in campaign speeches. Then, in a major strategic move, we faked the release of a tape telling how I conquered any woman I wanted. The county went nuts on that last one for the whole of two or three days while many of the men were laughing it up. On balance, it appears that I did well on the issue.

Health care. Of course I attacked everything that the prior President did during his administration. Easiest of all was finding fault with the health care plan that was so carefully put into play. I won on two fronts with this issue. First of all, very few people understood it. Fortunately for me, even those who had the greatest benefit from the plan didn't understand it. They simply got caught up in the noisy complaining of the Republican Party. Many of them voted for me because they didn't realize that a vote for me meant a vote toward taking away their health insurance.

The other front was the voters who feared that their in-place insurance policies would greatly increase in cost to support the plan. The Republicans were very effective in arguing that the health plan was bad for them and bad for the country, another case of less-than-superior intellect demonstrated by the American people. Of course, we collected virtually all of those votes.

Security fears. ICES has everyone concerned – keeping people up nights – about the threat of ICES to our country and the possibility of terrorist activities. Even though the last administration has done much to contain ICES and to protect us from terrorist attacks, crazy individuals who use ICES as an excuse still manage to shoot into crowds or set off explosives in populated areas. These people don't have a clue as to what ICES really is. They're deranged individuals who want their names in the paper, want to kill because they are hurting themselves, or see visions or hear voices. This fear was simple to grasp as a major issue with voters, so we talked tough. We told voters how we were going to wipe out ICES and protect our country. And so another multi-million votes came our way.

LGBTQ and the Disabled. I knew that my outrageous attitude toward people who have very little control of how they exist would bring laughs to my main target of voters – white, middle-class thugs. Naturally, this, too, gave me pages and pages of publicity. It's amazing that so-called prestigious media such as the New York Times and the New Yorker Magazine fell so hard for my tactics. They still do. What a joke. Then, by attacking media in general, I won many more voters.

My strategy was simple but obviously effective. Who would have thought that it would work?

Topic 18: Cutting Taxes

No one wants to pay taxes. They want government benefits but without paying taxes. I understand that, but we all know that it takes taxation to support our government's efforts and services. The question is who should pay and how much should they pay. I have definite views on this. I believe that the middle class should pay the bulk of taxes. They spend their money from paycheck to paycheck, so why not just build in taxes as one of the necessary costs right along with groceries, clothing, shelter, etc. You have to pay for what you get in this world; the middle class should pay a healthy percentage of their income because they receive a healthy percentage of benefits.

Those in the $150,000 all the way up to the millions bracket, however, should pay fewer taxes. I realize that sounds unfair at first blush, but let's look at the rationale. These are the people who invest in making our country work. We need investments to create jobs, to start new businesses, for research and development, and to pay the salaries of the ultra-qualified. Lower taxes for this group of money makers will result in more money for investments.

The idea of a graduated tax is nonsense. It is the rich who need to pay fewer taxes in order to have more money to make our country great. Sure, we can have military might, good schools, and outstanding citizens, but America is what it is because we have wealthy individuals who are willing to put their money where it will allow the country to grow. The wealthy need to be encouraged to invest by implementing a system of little or no taxes in their brackets. Why should they continue to search for ridiculous loopholes? Why not simply reduce or eliminate taxes of those in higher brackets?

Now, coincidentally, I happen to be a rich man, a very rich man. It is fortunate that my tax plan will increase my after-tax income considerably. Why shouldn't I take advantage of this small benefit of being the President of the United States? It is merely fortuitous that I am able to benefit by a tax plan that I will steer through Congress. It shouldn't be that difficult to do, since most Congressmen and Congresswomen are millionaires. That's how they got into Congress. I assure you that when I leave the Presidency, I will be even richer than when I became President. Why should it be any different? Have you ever heard of a politician going broke when in office? Somehow, somewhere there is always a financial benefit available.

I remember the case of Governor Jim Tomkernerwitz. Jim was a law professor when I first met him at a social gathering, but it was evident that he was a man on the rise.

Tomkernerwitz: Great pleasure to meet you, Donald. I've always envied your real estate know-how, your yachts, your sports cars, your wives, heh, heh.

Me: Well, I admire your audacity. How would you like a punch in the mouth?

Tomkernerwitz: Wouldn't do that if I were you, Donald. You see, as a law professor and a man who is about to be appointed the Federal Prosecutor for this region, I know a little about the consequences of assault and battery.

Me: Hmm, maybe we can negotiate a friendship after all.

Tomkernerwitz: Love to. Do you play tennis?

Me: Too busy making money, Jim, but I can see the possibility of our playing our games. I don't suppose that you've make a great deal of money as a law professor?

Tomkernerwitz: No, and that's where you can help, a little hand washing another, if you know what I mean.

It's true that it didn't take Tomkernerwitz that long to go from Federal Prosecutor to Governor, with my financial help, of course. And the relationship proved to be much more beneficial to me, also, considerably better than a punch in the mouth. Yes, after he sat in the Governor's Mansion, he became very useful in the information department. And he certainly didn't let opportunities go by neglected while he was in office. Mysteriously, he went from a poor law professor to a very wealthy man. Imagine that!

Topic 19: Nuclear Power

I have already said that as long as we have nuclear power, we should not hesitate to use it if necessary. In the meantime, until we decide when and if it is necessary, we need to continue to improve our nuclear capability through stockpiling and through research to make our weapons even more powerful. This tremendous power, when demonstrated by testing or by required use, will scare the hell out of every other potential nuclear power nation. When we are so far ahead of them that it is useless to attempt to catch up, other nations will simply give in to U.S. power.

The United States as well as many other nations has feared a race to develop superior nuclear power. Let's just win the 100 meter race by 50 meters. The others won't be able to compete. End of race.

Paradoxically, I do favor some nuclear power by countries that we can trust, countries that need our protection or countries where we are invested in their economic health. I'm talking South Korea because of the constant threat of North Korea and Japan because of its close economic ties. We might support a few others, considering circumstances at the time. Nevertheless, we have to be certain that they don't run past the 50 meter line while we're at the finish line.

Naturally, we should make every effort to assure that nuclear capability doesn't happen in some countries: North Korea, of course, but also China and any Mideast country. If our relationship with Russia continues to improve, I can see sharing some nuclear information with that country as long as it lags well behind us.

Now the other fear that the Nervous Neds have is that there will be a nuclear holocaust if someone accidentally triggers a nuclear attack. Do you really believe that someone is stupid enough to do that? Any nuclear arms would be treated with awe and care. And there has to be safeguards up the wazoo. No nation should have one individual who can press the button. That should be true of the United States as well as every other nation. In fact, the United States, after it has gained its enormous lead in developing nuclear capability, should be in the position to inspect any other nation's practices and safeguards if they have nuclear capability. I'll go farther than that: I think we should exercise our leadership by inspecting all countries to determine whether they have nuclear capability so that there are no surprises.

We have two choices when it comes to protecting the interests of Americans. First, we can do pretty much what we are doing now, that is to simply discourage nations from developing nuclear power. Or, two, we can do as I will encourage Congress to enable: provide the funding for all-out development by the United States so that no other country can possibly think of competing.

Once in a while, some two-bit country, North Korea or Iran, for example, brags about its ability to develop superior nuclear power with rockets that would reach the United States. That's when we have to step up to the plate and call their ridiculous bluffs. That's when we have to rattle not the sabers but the nuclear power available to us. Some claim that this is a dangerous policy. It isn't; it's the only policy. We have to shout louder and come out fighting if required.

Now while I have indicated that multiple individuals should be involved in the firing of nuclear weapons as a safeguard against accidents or mad men, of course in the United States, the President should have personal power. After all, if action is required, clearly there would be virtually no time to make a decision. While the President might seek input from trusted advisers, he and he alone (me, of course, in this administration) should have the final say.

This talk of nuclear power should not frighten anyone. Safety is in power, and power will always diminish threats. Americans will sleep more soundly knowing that its President is in full and final control.

Now, I want to tell you about a consideration that would involve nuclear power if absolutely required. That's when you have a mad man as the leader of a country. The Hitlers of this world should not happen and they and their closest allies should be forced to quit, to give up their power. Barney Paxmore had some thoughts on this:

Barney: People like Hitler and out-of-control dictators in the world today need to be stopped and I know how.

Me: What do you have in mind, Barney?

Barney: Why start wars that cause deaths and such misery for so many people? Simply, we need to eliminate those individuals, get rid of them before they can cause harm.

Me: And how do you propose to do that?

Barney: Money. We spend millions, if necessary. We bribe people close to these individuals to take them out. That would be a great bargain compared to what we would spend in all-out war, wouldn't it?

Me: So you think that there is always someone who will take money to do the deed.

Barney: Absolutely. If that doesn't work, then we send in our boys to do it. Surely, we can penetrate their defenses.

I have to tell you that Barney's a little nuts. We can't go after leaders like that. It would mean that other nations would go after our leaders. No, if it takes a war or even nuclear weapons, that's the way it has to be.

Topic 20. Tweeting

Franklyn Delano Roosevelt had fireside chats. He talked directly to the people on the radio. John Kennedy talked directly to the people on television because he had remarkable TV presence. I feel that tweeting is a valid and important form of communication. I LOVE to tweet. I can do it any time of the day or night, any time I feel the impulse.

Some people think that I go off half-cocked in some of my messages, but that's because they don't really know me. In fact, I deliberate every tweet very carefully. Whenever any of the millions who see my tweets read what I have to say, they know that it is often a proclamation of some kind or at least a considered opinion. I enjoy knowing that I have this immediate audience for whatever I have to say. Do you have any idea how many people sit at their computers or check their IPhones dozens of times a day? Millions and millions. Why should I worry about my appearance in front of a camera and why should I be committed to a certain time slot? No reason whatsoever as long as I can tweet. At 2:00 a.m. in the morning, I may have one of my many great ideas that I want to share or I'm lying awake because I have something on my mind that needs to be shared. Tweet. There is just something magical about reaching so many at the touch of my fingertips.

It's also a challenge, of course, to say exactly what I want to say in those 140 characters. It's better than playing scrabble.

That's a game I played often when I was younger. Of course, I cheated, use to go to the computer to find words that begin with x or short words that end in i. We always took breaks; that's when I did a little research without anyone being the wiser. I need to win at everything I do. It's just part of my genetic makeup. Now, my game is tweeting, and I usually manage to say exactly what I want to say, pretty much using all 140 characters. Okay, now the system lets me go over 140 characters. That was never really a limitation; I simply continued on to another tweet. Big deal.

Everyone's main concern seems to be that they don't have the opportunity to question me about whatever I've tweeted. It's not a press conference where a number of the media bark at me with their demanding questions. Well, I'll cover the media in a future segment. So the beauty of it is that it's entirely one-sided. If there are follow-up questions, too bad. If they want clarification of anything I've said, too bad. The downside, of course, is that I am sometimes misinterpreted, but I can always straighten that out with another tweet.

Many thought that I would give up tweeting when I became President. Why? Tweeting not only gives the opportunity to talk about serious, Presidential matters, it also allows me to give my opinion on which TV programs are most entertaining or who I think will win the Rose Bowl. Get used to it, everyone, because I'm going to tweet throughout my Presidency whenever I wish.

Topic 21: Solving World Problems

I want peace – in my country. Yes, I have advocated the improvement and use if necessary of nuclear weapons so that we are the most feared country in the world. Does that mean, however, that we need to step in every time there's a skirmish somewhere? In many instances, most for sure, we need to butt out. So what if the Jews can't get along with the Palestinians? Why should we interfere in battles between Middle East countries? Is it really important to us who the President is of Syria or Turkey? Why should we be the protectorate of South Korea or Afghanistan? Why is Turkey or Syria worth meddling in? I realize that my advisers will give me comprehensive answers to those questions, but let's pause and think some more about what's routinely happening, our involvement in those territories.

I don't see why we have to be the world's referee. Do we always have to decide who's right and then commit resources to support that side, sometimes even militarily? Hell, no! We need to look a whole lot harder at uprisings or sore feelings between nations. Clearly, often, we should not be involved in any way. It's their fight so let them determine who the winner is without outside participation.

Because of my friendship with Gobashitzen, I feel certain that I can keep Russia from meddling also. In the past, it has been the practice of large nations to interfere in what are domestic disputes. Oh, sure, there have been terrible killings – slaughters – that sometimes occur. I think that a stern warning from Russia and the United States should halt those practices. If they continue beyond what is reasonable to the situation, then of course a joint effort of both large powers could be necessary. Aleppo is one example of what might call for united action. It is not only the United States and Russia that have chosen sides in the past. Some other countries, particularly in the Middle East, have been prone to military bullying. The answer has to be cooperation among the sensible nations of this world to put a stop to unreasonable killing.

Another cause of consternation is geographic ambition. There is constantly some country that feels it has the right and power to grab off land from another country. Sometimes it starts with more-or-less innocent settlements in areas that do not clearly belong to the aggressive nation. Then we find ourselves deciding if these settlements are appropriate. Low and behold, the country initiating the settlements happens to be a close ally of the United States. Again, that puts us in the position of refereeing. Let the settlements take place. If this causes disruption between countries or religions, so be it. Surely it can work out without our participation as long as other countries stay out of the controversy.

I sincerely believe that if I had been President at the onset of World War II, I could have avoided all the bloodshed that took place. Hitler was a mad man, but Chamberlin had the right idea: talk him out of further aggression. Obviously, Chamberlin was not the negotiator that I am. I think that I would have found a way to curtail Hitler's ambitions. Of course we'll never know because that was long ago and we have freed our world of Hitlers. The point is that it is not necessary to stage all-out war when there are alternate answers, especially when we can negotiate from a position of immense nuclear power.

The long and the short of it is that it is my position to keep our country safe and to stay out of conflicts in countries when there isn't an absolute necessity of intervening.

Topic 22: The Media

Very much contrary to public opinion, I love the media. I also love Medea. Another joke. As you know, I love the media about as much as I love Medea. Anyway, what I began doing during the campaign I have continued into my Presidency. These people – the newspaper reporters and editors, the magazine writers, the television news stars – are suckers. I played them for all it's worth. Just take a look at virtually any newspaper on pages one, two, and three during the campaign. What do you see? My name in bold print two, three, four times. There's no way I could have purchased that kind of publicity without spending ten times the amount of money I spent during the campaign.

It was so easy. All I had to do was say something outrageous or make a pronouncement. They were all over whatever I said. It didn't matter to me how the article was written and for what purpose. If it was to discredit me or to minimize my campaign efforts, it didn't matter a whit. The important thing was it was there – day after day after day. Now if it was a positive article, fine. If it was negative toward me, fine. Most of the time, the articles weren't read. All that the newspaper subscriber saw was THUMP every day. Even if the article was negative, and was actually read, there is such mistrust of newspapers that the reader cheered for my side.

I'm not concerned with newspapers. They are, of course, obsolete. Ask ten people if they read a newspaper everyday and nine will tell you no. If pressed on the issue, they will say that they read the news off their smart phones. In truth, it is highly unlikely that they read the news there either. What we have is a population that cares little about the news. Earlier generations sat and read the newspaper every day, religiously. Some older Americans still do that, but not many. No one really has the time or interest to sit and read the newspaper today, unless they take a quick look at the headlines, the sports page, the obits, and the comics. Newspapers will no longer be with us ten or twenty years from now. Sure, you will have the selective few – the Washington Post, the New York Times – but they'll be sold primarily for the crossword puzzles. The average day for an editor will be to find some controversial consequence that can be pinned on me. The average day for a reporter will be to look for other employment.

Magazines? The number of magazines continues to grow, but the items are about sex (headlines that say 100 Ways to Make Your Special Friend Hot or 100 Newly Discovered Sex Techniques), food, fashion, cars, or history. The news magazines have a shrinking subscription base. By the time the magazine reaches the reader, the news items are no longer news and the editorial comment is stale, having already been chewed over by the TV and radio guys. Maybe Time should stick to a whole magazine of letters from their readers (the most interesting pages of the magazine) and maybe New Yorker should stick to the cartoons and poetry that no one understands.

Now we get to the crème the resistance: the TV networks. Does CNN really stand for Culpably Nutty Network? They talked, talked about me night and day throughout the campaign and since the beginning of my Presidency. One minute it's a hard fact item, then the next minute it's rumor, the next it's speculation and innuendo. It could have gone to my head, but I just got bored with the whole thing. All the time, though, they kept my name and image in front of the public. While they ventured to give opinions why I won the election, all they had to do was look at what they helped accomplish by giving me constant exposure. I love the way they have four, five, six, whatever reporters trying to outshout each other and mug the camera at the same time. Delicious. I am especially amazed at the way a CNN newscaster never lets anyone answer a question before another question is asked. Let them answer the question you asked, for Pete's sake. The interviewee may actually have something to say. No, it's all about them, not the person who is being interviewed.

Fox does its best to be different. The way that is accomplished theoretically is to support me when everyone else is clearly against me. Unfortunately, Fox is a second-rate CNN, a copycat, a minor leaguer. I give Fox the impression that we're buddies, just so I can get all that support that they are so anxious to give me, but come on. There's no talent there, either. All the rest are there hoping against hope that somebody out there is watching.

Oh yeah, the Correspondents Dinner. What a joke that is. There is no way that I was going to be there to take the punches. Of course, the idea is to give the President an opportunity to retaliate with a small requirement that he do it humorously. Maybe that worked for the prior President or for guys who had good joke writers. I don't have any clowns on my staff; we're all too busy – and sometimes we're so busy because we're fighting off accusations by the press. No, let them have the Correspondents Dinner without the President. Let them stuff that into their chicken dinners.

Anyway, every time I insult the media, a feeding frenzy ensues. They're incredibly easy. The newspapers and magazines will probably print this book in its entirety in daily or weekly installments. Yeah, I love the media.

Topic 23: My Inauguration

What a ball! Actually, what a number of balls. Of course, the balls were entertaining, but the main event came earlier in the day. Donald Thump was sworn in as President of the United States. I must say that the former President was gracious about it; he really believes that transfer of power is one of the great assets of our country. Anyway, it went very well. All those people out there worshiping ME. Easily, I would estimate that there were more people at this inauguration than any inauguration in history. I was sworn in by the Chief Justice, of course. We had a nice lead-in with The Ripe Tomatoes Rock Band and a poem by the Poet Laureate, whoever that was. And the parade was sensational, a wonderful reminder to the world that the new President has arrived.

I have to tell you that one of the highlights of my inauguration day was planking one of the most beautiful women I've ever seen. It happened at one of the balls. With the way everyone was surrounding me wherever I went, it's just amazing that this happened. Her name was Gabrielle. Somehow, she managed to get a one-on-one with me by convincing everyone that she had to see me in private because of information she had, something I needed to know. Of course, that was patently foolish, but when I heard it, I was intrigued. Add to that her outstanding beauty, probably the most beautiful woman I've ever seen, and it was irresistible to have my secret service guy find me a private room.

When Gabrielle came on to me so aggressively but gracefully, she was difficult to resist. Then, I thought, hell, this is something no incoming President ever did, ever. We went at it for maybe ten minutes because that's all the time I could spare. It may very well be that she'll be a visitor at the White House sometime. I'll think about it. Those Secret Service guys really do provide secret service.

Of course, I really enjoyed the swearing in ceremony. I have never seen so many people in one place. An incredible number of people were there at the Inauguration, clearly way more than were present for any other President's Inauguration ceremony. I guess I said that but it's worth repeating. I just don't know how many streets and alleys were filled with people wanting to be close to the Inauguration, even though many could not really see or hear the event. Clearly, my election instigated more enthusiasm and excitement by just regular Americans than ever before.

I'll always remember the activities of that day – all of them.

Topic 24: Senator Carl Stewart

Where is this guy coming from? He's been a thorn in my side since the election. He's criticized every statement I've made. Of course, I expect that to some degree. He's a Democrat after all. Nevertheless, he's intense. He's getting under my skin for sure.

What am I supposed to do, just ignore him? That's difficult to do when the press is listening to him and giving him unnecessary coverage. We all know that he gets that attention because (1) he's been in the Senate for 30 years, (2) he's black, and (3) he marched right along with Martin Luther King. Does that exempt him from my responding to his gibes? I don't think so.

So I put it to him before I became President and I haven't let up and won't let up until he gets off my back. The thing is that I'm the President now and he's still just one of 100 senators. Let's see who wins this battle.

As I've said repeatedly I am not a racist. However, I do feel that we've opened too many doors to Blacks with their aggressive, vengeful nature. I say vengeful because I feel that many of them are still trying to get even for the treatment of their ancestors. That was unfortunate but not the fault of the modern white man. Sometimes I wish that we never changed that three-fifths rule that applied to voting, a Black getting only a three-fifths vote. Instead we've gone all out for equality. It's not working, folks.

Right away, of course, I was criticized for denouncing the fool. He simply doesn't understand that Blacks have been slowing down the progress of the country. Yes, we want to give them opportunities but they've defaulted. Take Senator Stewart, for example. He was elected again and again by his constituents because the state is primarily black and they manage to get out the vote for him. He doesn't deserve to be in Congress. He's there because he's black in a black state. How is that any accomplishment? I have no idea why I need to respect that. I'll say whatever I want about him whenever I want. I have the feeling that I will be respected for standing up to him. It's a general consensus that I will need the Black vote time and again during my four years on this job, but enough is enough.

Many have said that I need this guy to stay on the right side of the Black Caucus. Are they kidding me? I intend to exercise full control over all aspects of federal government. If anyone thinks that one group of Congressmen can get in my way, there is a large misunderstanding of the power I plan to assume in my duties as President of the United States.

Topic 25: Women's March

Talk about a bunch of poor losers. The claim is that there were hundreds of thousands of women (and some of their lackey husbands and boyfriends) "marching" (more likely loitering) in several big cities protesting the fact that I became President. What? I watched some of it on TV. What a joke! For the little time I watched, I saw half a dozen lesbians shaking their bodies for emphasis while they said nothing important. All right, not everyone was a lesbian. Some were shaking their big boobs because they want the right to kill babies. Yeah, yeah, you have a right to your own body. If women didn't give up their bodies so easily, they wouldn't have to be so concerned with what happens to their bodies afterward.

Here's what's going to happen: No one is going to remember the women march nonsense for very long. They will go back to their petty jobs and nestled families and simply give up whatever they were protesting. I don't know exactly what they were protesting and I don't want to know, so they accomplished nothing if they thought that I was going to listen to a horde of shouting women.

I have no problem with women. I love women. Many of them are my good friends. I think that women should have every opportunity that a man has. (Well, maybe not sports color commentator. Those women down on the field during a football game just don't belong. Other than eye candy, do they really accomplish anything?). The demonstrating women just saw an opportunity to act out and to call attention to themselves. When they see all that I am going to do for this country, they will change their tunes. I know they want to talk about women's rights, maybe LGBTQs, but they'll find out how fair and creative I can be about these issues. I think that they'll come around eventually, probably in a month or two.

Topic 26: NATO

What's it stand for? Not All That Obvious? I know it stands for National Atlantic Treaty Organization or something like that. I just don't care. NATO has been shafting us from day one and it's about time that we do something about it.

First, let's look at what NATO has accomplished. Nothing. It's made up of 28 countries, including the United States, with this outdated concept that an attack on any member nation is an attack on all of them. That's just dandy for these small countries that can't defend themselves. That puts them in the position of the United States protecting them. What do they do for the United States? That's where the nothing comes in. We don't need their help. They need us. The short of it is that we put ourselves in this situation way back in 1949 just after World War II when we had the Marshall Plan and we were putting ourselves out to protect everyone else after a tremendous war victory. And that's where it stands: 27 countries being protected by us and we don't need their protection.

All of this protection and consultation activity costs money. We have this idea of collective defense (spelled defence in the agreement; why can't these people spell?). We are on the hook to consult and encourage cooperation to bring about peaceful resolution of disputes. Yeah, Latvia will be there to help resolve disputes. And who's footing the bill for all of this protection and consultation? The United States, of course. As soon as I get around to it, we're going to take a look at how much we're spending and how much Latvia is spending.

As long as I'm giving thought to NATO, I might as well re-examine the other organizations that look to us for aid all the time. Yes, I'm talking about the United Nations. What has it accomplished? Here's another outfit that's bleeding us dry financially. How many members of the U.N. have paid dues and expenses? I'm going to take a good look at that. And how many members have participated with military assistance when needed? We needed help in Vietnam. We fought the North Vietnamese with a group called the United Nations forces, but we all know those were primarily American forces on the ground.

There's a new administration in the United States and we'll see about our involvement in NATO AND the United Nations.

Topic 27: Ku Klux Klan

The Klan, as it's called, started way back in the 1860s in an attempt to maintain white supremacy. It kicked in again in the 1920s, this time in answer to the immigration of Catholics and Jews from Eastern Europe. Once in a while, you hear that the Klan is still in existence. Methods used by the Klan involved intimidation through violence and even murder. They wore those ridiculous costumes that looked like bed sheets and cones with slits so they could see where they were going. They weren't going anywhere after laws were passed to take care of the problem in the 1860s and the laws were enforced during the trouble in the 1920s. Supposedly, the Klan made another comeback in the 1960s during the civil rights laws during that period, again aimed at African Americans. In reality, that wasn't the Klan; that was just a number of deranged Whites who wanted to teach some lessons, even if the recipients of those lessons were white civil rights workers.

I believe that the Klan ended its genuine scare tactics in the 1860s. Everything since then has been a joke. No one takes the Klan seriously anymore. Any time you put together anti-black vigilante groups, disgruntled poor white farmers, displaced Democratic politicians, illegal whiskey distillers, conservative moral reformers, sadists, rapists, or common thieves, you have the possibility of a Ku Klux Klan rebirth.

Oddly, I can almost understand the need for such an organization. Those who are displaced in the society through government laws and by changes in social acceptances must have an outlet. Of course, I do not condone violence of any kind, but I do see that there could be social clubs of this sort, even with ridiculous costumes. If they act out without creating actual harm, I see no reason to discourage such behavior. I might even encourage this behavior as therapeutic.

It's true that I did talk to KKK leader David Puke during the election.

Puke: Donald, there is a need for dissension because we have gotten carried away with granting equality to individuals who are not the kind of individuals we want in this country.

Me: Now hold on, David, we are way past the time we want to openly discriminate against Blacks.

Puke: No, I'm not talking about Blacks, although the Klan would be happy to see them all shipped back to Africa.

Me: Now, David, don't let that movie remake of Birth of a Nation influence you. It's too late to send the Catholics and the Jews back to Eastern Europe.

Puke: Not them either, although our organization wouldn't mind if we had a whole lot fewer Catholics and Jews in this country. You have no idea how hard we have worked for the purification of American society. All those burning crosses scared the hell out of them.

Me: Who, then?

Puke: The immigrants, the refugees, of course; they're coming from all over the world, especially the Middle Eastern countries. We don't want them now any more than we wanted the Negroes, the Irish, the Polacks, or the Jews. With you in office, maybe Congress won't lean so hard on us if we lead the way to obstruct that flow into the United States.

Me: Hmm, maybe you have something there. Somebody has to do something about that problem and that somebody is me, but a little help from the Klan wouldn't hurt. Do you still have to wear those stupid costumes?

Puke: I'll have to think about that, Donald. You know that's a fine tradition. Those costumes are scary. Tell you what, Donald, why don't I come out for you in this election. We'll let all the Klan members and all the discontents in the country know that we're for you.

Me: Ah, let me think about that.

Okay, maybe it is a really dumb organization, but a little anti-Black, anti-Catholicism, and anti-Semitism can't be all bad.

Topic 28: Vaccinations

I don't particularly trust doctors, especially the ones who do research. It bothers me that so much money goes to some of these research organizations, mostly private funds but also considerable government funds. We've been contributing to cancer research for years and we still have cancer. We've been contributing to diabetes research for years and we still have diabetes. The slogan is always about looking for a cure. However, some of the executives of these organizations make a ton of money while there is no cure in sight. I also don't trust the pharmaceutical companies. Drug costs have skyrocketed while doctors continue to prescribe more and more drugs.

Do the doctors and the pharmaceutical companies really want a cure for some of the major diseases? I wonder. Take diabetes. The doctors need to see their diabetes patients at least two or three times a year just for a quick check-up with a resulting bill to the patient or to Medicare. The pharmaceutical companies sell testing equipment and test strips, insulin, oral medication, diabetic socks, and other paraphernalia that diabetics are convinced they need. Do they really want all those sales to go out the window? Anyway, let's get to vaccinations.

There is a rush to get everyone vaccinated for everything. You can go by your local drug store and get vaccinations for just about anything. You can pay on the spot or they'll bill Medicare for you. It's a wonder they haven't figured out how to do them through the drive-thru. How about the dangers of piling all of these vaccinations on the worried consumer? One really strange aspect of all of those vaccinations being performed by drug stores is that there is utter confusion in those stores. One of my friends, Barney Playitsafe, told me about his trip to a drug store to inquire into a vaccination for shingles.

Barney: You see, my wife came down with shingles, just a very limited version but shingles nevertheless. Her doctor told her that I should get vaccinated against shingles because, of course, I had been exposed to her.

Me: Makes sense.

Barney: Well, not so much. I've never had chicken pox, but here I go thinking I needed the shot. So I go to the drug store and see signs there that promote vaccinations, especially flu and shingles shots. Then I see in the information flyer right there on the counter that shingles is not infectious. I ask the pharmacist and he says, "Well, you can get one just to be on the safe side." Okay, I say, will my Medicare cover it? "I don't know," he says, "you'll have to ask your insurance company."

Me: So you didn't get the shot?

Barney: Well, I push him on the Medicare thing and he does a computer search that takes twenty minutes. In the meantime, another pharmacist is looking for the vaccine. She stands up on a ladder to reach a refrigerator, but it's locked. Then she asks around and finds out that the key to the refrigerator is locked in a different refrigerator.

Me: Are you serious? That's how they keep the vaccine?

Barney: Yeah, even though they have big signs that they give vaccinations, they have to scout around for a while to find the stuff.

Me: Okay, so did you get the shot or didn't you?

Barney: I had to sign a few forms and give them some personal information before they reached for the vaccine. But then, the guy on the computer tells me that Medicare and my supplement insurance won't cover the entire cost.

Me: So you had to reach into your pocket.

Barney: Not me, not when they told me how much I would have to pay in addition to what Medicare and my insurance was paying. Two hundred thirty-three bucks. Forget it, I said, I'll take my chances.

There is still considerable controversy over whether vaccinations can cause autism. You see all kinds of reports that deny this but facts are facts. In 1990 one out of every 10,000 children was autistic. Now, it's one in about 150. Why? Changing climate conditions, nuclear plants? No, the real variable is vaccinations. Many trust-worthy medical experts claim that it can't be proven that vaccinations don't cause autism. Worse, there are instances of brain swelling, seizures, and blood diseases all directly attributable to vaccinations. My friend, eminent physician Harvey Wolfgang Knowslittle, spoke to me about his concern with vaccinations.

Knowslittle: My concern is that those vaccine developers are taking short cuts to get their names in the medical journals before their colleagues. Therefore, they are making vaccines that are greatly contaminated.

Me: Wouldn't the FDA put a stop to that?

Knowslittle: I think the FDA didn't want to cause undue concern for parents, so it was full-speed ahead to see who could get there first for any number of vaccines, even though they knew there was contamination. What's a little contamination being injected into your blood stream?

Me: Wouldn't the word get out by now how unsafe vaccines are?

Knowslittle: Well, you know, most of those scientists are German. When they see each other and say vos ist los, they reply der hound ist los. Know what I mean?

Me: No, but I'm going to do something about it now that I'm President.

I also had a conversation with my friend Bobby Shivers:

Me: Bobby, you're a healthy guy, still playing tennis at 92. How do you account for your excellent condition at your age?

Bobby: I stay at home a lot so that I'm not exposed to all those germs that seem to float around everywhere. Oh, and I avoid vaccinations. The last one I had was when I was 19. I haven't had one since. There is no way that I am going to expose myself to the ignorance and carelessness that surrounds vaccinations.

I've decided to issue an Executive Order that will stop all vaccinations until the FDA has had an opportunity to conduct new research into the side effects and consequences of such injections. The investigation will be intense but for a short period so as not to prevent vaccinations that are truly needed.

Topic 29: Pipelines

We can really boost employment with pipelines. I'm for removing all restraints on building them wherever there's a need. Sure, the employment will be mostly temporary, but temporary is good in large numbers, and it sure will look good in reducing the unemployment rate figures early in my administration. We're talking thousands of good-paying jobs.

I recognize that the pipelines are not only for oil but to carry some sludge products also, but that doesn't impact the fact that we will be putting people to work. It's even better, I believe, that there is some concern about leakage and poisoning water. Why? Because that requires more workers to be certain that the pipelines are built with sturdy, safe material so that won't happen.

I know that there are areas where demonstrations have taken place against the building of the pipeline, North Dakota, for example. I think it's been some time since we've asked for opinions on governing from the Indians (whoops, the Native Americans). We have to do what's best for the whole of the country, not for an ancient civilization. Here's the deal: The Native Americans can demonstrate to their heart's content, along with all those other disrupters who demonstrate for the joy of demonstrating, and I'm going to turn a deaf ear. I know what's good for this country. The pipelines will be built through Tampa if I think that turns out to be a good place for them.

Topic 30: Trade Agreements

First, we get rid of the Trans Pacific Partnership. It provides great economic breaks for our friends the Japanese but doesn't do a hill of beans for us. The idea, mostly, is to allow free use of ports in the partner countries. Yeah, we need that. Goods are going to flow through our ports a zillion more times than through those other ports. It's going, going, gone in the very near future. The TPP is going to become the TP as far as I'm concerned. Get it?

There are just too many fucking trade agreements: NATO, the European Union, the World Trade Organization, etc. I say get rid of them all. They're sucking the blood out of the United States and we are willing suckees. All right, NATO does more than provide trade opportunities, but I'm ticked because they don't pay their way. How many times can I say that?

The British were so smart to get out of the Common Market. The people knew best just as I proved when I was elected, at least the people who managed to give me enough electoral votes. As you know, I'm still annoyed at all those other votes that obviously were fraudulent.

Anyway, we don't need trade agreements. They hurt the American worker with too many goods manufactured elsewhere that find their way here without paying the import fees that should be paid. We're going to take care of that.

All right, maybe I caved a bit on this issue as my Presidency began. It would have helped if I had more information about what all those groups do and whether, in fact, they're good for our country. Of course I was accustomed to acting on what was good for my bank account. Turns out that some of the organizations actually provide some benefit to most everyone's bank account. Anyway, I've put my financial guys on it. We'll make a decision on what action we'll take in regard to the trade organizations in the near future.

Topic 31: The CIA

There's a contradiction of terms. I've never seen such a screwed up agency. I think the people who have been working for the Central Intelligence (yeah!) Agency have seen too many movies about the CIA. What we really have is not the guys who accomplish so much in the movies but a bunch of white-shirt-and-tie guys who majored in accounting and somehow think they're accomplished 007s. Oh, I praised them when I first took office. Now, I'm slowly going to dissect them, starting at the top. Of course, I have my own man as Chief, Herbert Doover (pronounced do over).

The CIA is supposed to know what is going on all over the world, especially in those countries that might be a threat to the United States in any way. We found out that they didn't know beans about what was going on in the Middle East. Hell, an organization that is clearly a threat to world peace was created and built while the CIA was napping. We can't have that. I need to know exactly what's happening all over the world so I can make military and trade decisions that will bring about deterrence.

Maybe there are too many military and former military staff members at the CIA. Fortunately, I l can look at it from a civilian point of view. Military guys always want to suggest military solutions to problems. That's all right, but we need to look at the whole picture. That's what I can do. That's why I have been such a success in the business world, my ability to have total perspective.

It was no secret that I was going to shake up the CIA when I appointed Doover who used to be an undercover guy as well as a writer, kind of like a Jack Ryan. He'll be in close touch with the President, me, at all times. No action will be taken by the CIA without my specific approval. Consequently, I'll be on top of any staff appointments – and there will be many. We're going to have a CIA that will be wonderful, one that will work very well.

And I won't even talk about the other elephant in the room right now, the FBI Director. I'm still thinking what to do about him. Send him packing maybe?

Topic 32: Torture

I believe in torture to get information out of enemy personnel. When you think about how some of these groups cut off heads and commit all kinds of atrocities, why should we pussyfoot around using torture as a device for getting helpful facts about what the enemy is doing? Water boarding has been the most discussed with people saying that water boarding is cruel. Of course it's cruel. That's why it works. It puts panic and desperation in the hearts and minds of the person being tortured, so the information comes pouring out.

Once again on this issue, you have people and organizations objecting to torture of all kinds. They say that our country believes in humanity and fairness. Just think about the losses on 9/11 and about other terrorist attacks that might have been prevented if we looked for better information, information that might have been attained if some were convinced to tell what they knew. We let opportunities go by when we do not utilize torture.

I will go one step farther as to whether torture should be used. I believe it should be allowed by all legitimate police authority, that they should be extensively trained on how to use torture in getting criminals to confess. If this requires a Constitutional Amendment, so be it. Let's get the scum off the streets and into prison cells.

Topic 33: Big City Murders

They've got to stop. Too many gang fights and too many people who do not fear murder sentences. We need to declare martial law in some of the cities until we can get the murder rate under control. We are going to investigate two possible solutions:

1. We need to have capital punishment reinstated in all states but starting with the big cities where most murders have occurred. I think that the electric chair was effective in carrying out capital punishment, none of this business of gas devices that are often troublesome. The image of someone frying in an electric chair is the image that we want out there for criminals to see and remember when they consider murdering someone. When a person dies in the electric chair, it accomplishes two goals: that person is no longer a danger to society and that person becomes an example of what will happen to anyone else who commits murder. Of course, we'll have the Civil Liberties Union and the teary hearts on us because of reinstating capital punishment, but they should know that our hope is to protect everyone, including them, from losing a brother, sister, mother, or father to a murdering beast. Even if the bleeding hearts continue to put down the electric chair as an

effective method to reduce murders in this country, I will recommend frontal lobotomies, something that was very popular in this country long ago to stabilize the violently mentally ill. In my book, anyone who commits murder is violently mentally ill, so let the punishment fit the crime.

2. We need federal forces sent to big cities with high murder rates to remain until the problem is solved. I will ask Congress for funds to train special forces as well as to train National Guardsman to patrol gang-ridden areas. They will be instructed to shoot first and answer questions later. This will keep gangs of young men and women off the streets.

Criminals understand only if force is used. No more of this reducing sentences for good behavior and no more pampering of criminals. We're going to toughen up our prisons also. No more country clubs. If all that criminals understand is force, then we will use force.

I especially like the stance of my new Chief Gang Fighter, a position that I created to take action in big cities.

Werner DerFastfinger: We will meet them in the streets, in the alleys, in the sewers, wherever murderers go. They will be gunned down if necessary but captured alive for the electric chair whenever possible. We'll not only see to it that gang members are brought to justice but we will go after men and women who kill their spouses, executives who kill their bosses, and jealous lovers who kill in a rage.

Me: That sounds very comprehensive.

DerFastfinger: Warm up the electric chairs and start training the sharpshooters because here vee come.

Me: Vee?

DerFastfinger: Ya, here vee come.

Topic 34: Ethics

I've had all this bitching about not giving up all of my assets now that I'm President of the United States. What the hell???? I worked long and hard for my riches, so why should I just put them in the hands of some nobody. Do I look like an idiot? Sure, I guess Presidents in the past have put their assets in what is called a blind trust. That means that someone will take care of them and I will have no influence. That's nuts.

I intend to be certain that I don't become a pauper during my Presidency. The problem is that no President in the past has ever had my billions, yes billions. I'm confident that I can continue to run my financial empire while I am President. I have no intention of taking advantage of my Presidency by making large profits by steering government funds toward my investments nor do I intend to create government programs that will directly benefit my finances. So I'm a liar. Of course I'm going to ignore all those ethics that require totally ignoring personal gain during this very powerful opportunity. Screw ethics. My holdings and investments are so extensive that it would be a miracle if there wasn't an intertwining of decisions made by me and the fact that my personal wealth would continue to soar.

Here I am one of the richest men in the world and, at the same time, the most powerful man in the world. Ethics is for school boys, not men like me. You know that there is right and wrong, but how those terms are defined depends on such things as the wealth or lack of wealth of the individuals being evaluated as ethical or not ethical. For a man like me, ethics is nonsense. You can't measure ethics when it comes to the President of the United States, a man who has attained such success financially. Let the poor and the mediocre talk about ethics. For me, the word has no meaning.

Topic 35: Bank Regulations

Look around you in any city or town. You'll see banks, sometimes located in a small building, sometimes located in vast structures. The reason is simple: banks know how to make money. They use the money of every depositor and everyone who has a checking account. They lend those dollars to individuals at profitable rates. They invest those dollars. Through the magic of utilizing your money, they amass money. Is this good for the economy? Of course it is.

However, along comes government to interfere with how banks are run. Roosevelt shut down all the banks during the Depression. He had to for a short period just to prevent everyone from taking their money out of the banks and shutting down these important institutions for good. But later governments went too far in restricting the activities of banks, passing laws that require rules and regulations of how certain activities should be carried out. These laws seriously restricted the ability of banks to take advantage of what can be done with all those deposit dollars, all those checking accounts, all those loans.

This is just another example of over-reaching by government. It shouldn't happen, especially with institutions as important as banks. I say let the banks operate without restrictions in a free market. If banks are successful, businesses will be successful.

Opponents to freeing banks from tight restrictions point to how banks failed in prior years or how banks were too careless in making loans, not requiring real proof that the loans could be prepaid. This was competition. and competition is always good for an economy. So we're going to see to it that all those laws and all those rules and regulations go by the wayside. We're going back to banks making money and banks making money for businesses.

Now, I'm a smart guy – a very smart guy – but sometimes I take advice anyway from an expert. I talked to Werner Buffy, the man who knows everything about financing.

Me: Werner, what's with all these bank regulations?

Buffy: We have to look at the entire financial picture before we can determine the place of banks in our economy.

Me: Yes, and …

Buffy: We need banks. Where would I put all my money if we didn't have banks? And, as it happens, I own a few of the better banks.

Me: So you would not want to restrict bank activity in any way, right?

Buffy: You are so right. If you look at the graphs I've prepared for you here, you will see that the green arrow indicating free trade for banks far surpasses the red arrow indicating tightly controlled banks. Put some of your money in banks, Donald, and I'm not talking piggy banks.

Topic 36: Judges

Since I took over as President of the United States, I've run into one serious stumbling block to providing what I think is good for America: federal judges. They're all over the damn place getting in my face. I issue a perfectly sound executive order and it's questioned by some pipsqueak of a federal judge. I push a law through and some do-good organization brings suit to declare it unconstitutional in Federal Court.

I know that these judges have been appointed by Presidents, including some Republican Presidents, but it's time that we take a look at this business of life appointments. Some of them are senile and some are just incompetent. Yet there they are sitting in judgment of my efforts. A life appointment is a big mistake. What we need is a periodical review of the work and health of federal Judges to determine whether they should continue to serve. This needs to be done by an objective source, one appointed by the President. If this requires a Constitutional Amendment, so be it. It would be worth the effort to get rid of some so called judges.

There is no way that some 80-year-old should be sitting in judgment of what is and isn't Constitutional. Many of these guys are over the hill and still sit with all that power. We can't get them to quit unless we can prove that that they've committed treason or something serious like that. Hell, there was one Federal Appellate Court Judge who was writing his opinions in verse!

I'll be looking into revised methods of selecting judges and looking at this lifetime appointment business. It is my belief that any sitting President should be able to replace a federal judge at will. After all, the President appoints the judges, so why can't he dismiss them?

Again, we're going to hear from the whining law professors that it is the intention of the Constitution to establish safeguards by not placing all of the power with the President but, instead, providing for Judicial and Legislative branches. That's a problem that needs fixing; the President needs more power to carry out his decisions and not have to put up with obstacles placed in front of him by judges.

Topic 37: The Environment

A former Vice-President and Presidential candidate produced a movie about the dangers of global warming. I sat through half of it. It didn't bring tears to my eyes; it brought nausea to my stomach. What a lot of baloney. Some people are getting all choked up about what might happen to our planet in 2099. Yeah, I'm going to worry about that. With all the craziness in this world, none of us may be here in 2099.

I'm a man who wants to use whatever technical progress we've made. That means full steam ahead with modern technology. It also means that we should use all of the natural resources that are available. Why are we saving them? Use coal, use oil, use electricity. We have harnessed strength and power; let's put them to good use. Yes, there are downsides, but we can live with those negatives.

One of my first acts was to straighten out some people at the Environmental Protection Agency. More and more damn rules and regulation existed within that department. Some were forced on the agency by Congress or by Executive Orders coming from a prior President, but that doesn't mean the agency had to get fanatical about carrying out those restrictions.

We have dealt with the problems of our time. Why can't we let future generations deal with their problems? Government and private industry know what problems have to concern us in our generation. We are smart enough to take care of those concerns. There is every reason in the world to believe that if the air gets poisoned or if there is depletion of natural resources, the future generations will handle those problems. Get it? We deal with problems as they arise, so when the problems hit a future generation, they will work to solve them. It is not our job to handle the problems of the future.

Topic 38: Family Businesses

I have a very smart family, very smart. Dunkin and Mellow worked with me in my business empire and now, as you know, they have special jobs in the administration. That will not prevent them from being the entrepreneurs they continue to be. While they worked for my worldwide businesses, both of them initiated businesses of their own. Dunkin created an S Corporation devoted to improving the flow of goods through drone delivery. He now has over 10,000 drones in operation.

Mellow has always had a flair for creating shoe designs for children. Her website draws retail operations as well as individual shoppers. Just recently, she began initiating new designs for teenagers.

Although both now work in this Administration, I see no reason why they can't continue to spend part of their time in their personal operations. After all, like their Dad, they put in 16-18 hours a day. That should be rewarded.

Marketing efforts will always be dear to the hearts of both Dunkin and Mellow. They enjoy the biff-bang quality of selling their products and services. Of course, the constant presence they will have with me as President won't hurt business. What better advertising than just to be in front of the cameras all the time. They may even mention their companies and how their products or services can be obtained while discussing governmental issues with the press. I know some people will object to these marketing opportunities, claiming that it's unethical to occupy a government position while continuing private efforts – and doing a bit of marketing as a crossover – but that's exactly what they did before joining the Administration by running their own companies while working for me.

I have trained my children to make money. They will pursue that goal while I'm President. If being President helps them in any way, so be it.

Deborah has and will continue to be attacked, I suppose, because she has opted to continue her modeling career on a limited basis. Clearly, she still makes a startlingly beautiful presence and wears clothes at great advantage. At first, we thought about her modeling only for not-for-profit efforts, but she received so many requests to participate in some of the better shows that she decided to continue her career in modeling. As you know, I think women should be able to do whatever they want as far as careers go. Why should I limit her activities just because she is now First Lady? I imagine that she will be drawing large audiences of buyers and that the brands she models will do very well.

It is true that on a few occasions members of my staff mentioned Dunkin's efforts or Mellow's company, and it is true that the kids have been criticized for continuing their money making efforts. I have stayed out of that controversy, but I will tell you that I think that's really getting picky. If they happen to be enthusiastic about these companies and accidentally blurt out some support for them, that shouldn't be a big thing. I mentioned this issue to my friend Charles Chasez.

Me: Charles, you've been in the perfume business for years. I bet you took every opportunity to promote your scents, even when you were the French Ambassador to the United Nations.

Chasez: Mais, of course, mon ami. A good marketer always finds opportunities to inform possible consumers.

Me: Were the French people critical of your carrying those samples around the U.N.?

Chasez: Mais non. The French are a very understanding people. Anything that can result in amour, you know, is perfectly tres bonne.

So, if an Ambassador to the U.N. believes that any job, including a government one, can be used to promote a business, why should I dispute it?

And then there I am with my personal wealth, far greater than any past President. I didn't become this rich because I am foolish. All of this talk about my giving up my businesses to serve as President is ridiculous. If it happens that my wealth grows simply because foreign governments curry favor by offering my companies handouts or because foreign banks will scramble to finance my many enterprises simply because I am President of the United States, so be it. Enough said.

Topic 39: Why I Continue to be a Winner

I've told you why I won the election way back in Topic 17. The amazing thing is that I'm still popular with the people who elected me. Forget the rest. I made promises during the campaign and I am keeping them as President. All those white voters who fear outsiders, whether they are Mexicans or Muslims, are still with me. All those gun-totters are happy; they can buy rapid fire weapons at a moment's notice. All those folks who were concerned about their insurance rates going up because of the prior President's health plan are relaxed (for the moment). All those guys who didn't like the idea of a woman becoming President succeeded in a getting a real man. All those guys who secretly admired my way with women see that I still have my stuff, which also means that I don't have sympathy or concern for all the LGBTQ voters who didn't want me in office. All those non-sleepers who were up nights because they feared ICES now know that I am not reluctant to do whatever is necessary to handle that danger.

And so I am what the big white block expected: their President. However, I happen to be everyone's President, so the rest of the country just has to suck it up. And anyone who thinks I am going to change one iota because I am now in this unique position will be disappointed. As Popeye used to say, "I yam what I yam."

What is truly amazing is that one reason I am still popular with the people who elected me to office is that I'm rich. Simply,

I'm enormously wealthy. Voters keep putting rich people in office as Governors, Congressmen, and now President. That was certainly one of the reasons John F. Kennedy was elected. Lyndon Johnson had some bucks, too. It is a mystery to me why voters think that wealthy people make good leaders. Maybe they believe that the wealthy Governor, Congressman, or President will make the state or country wealthier through better economic decisions. Maybe they feel that the elected candidate will share his wealth somehow. Or maybe there is just something really attractive about a rich person, something that is admired by the average Joe.

I'm going to stay popular with the people who put me in office because I will remain the person my voters wanted and respected. I'll satisfy them as best I can and look forward to the next election and an additional four years as President.

Topic 40: My Boca Estate

I've enjoyed the Florida weather and people for over twenty years. I have this palatial winter home in Boca Raton. I had the home built shortly after I read in New Yorker Magazine that one out of every ten homeowners in Boca is a millionaire. So I thought why not have a billionaire among them? Those are the people I enjoy the most, people who have made it big time. I don't have to be concerned about my neighbors hustling me – or even being rude to me. My winter home looks out over the beach and the ocean, a private beach of course. I didn't buy the ocean.

Now that I am President, I will be hosting any number of foreign guests at the Thump Winter Palace, I call it. This will be an opportunity to impress the guests with my way of living and with how a country such as the United States provides opportunities unparalleled in history. I won't mind that using my home to host guests will also allow me to have the government pay for all expenses in connection with those visits. Why not? I've already established a precedent in profiting from foreign governments and businesses paying rent to live in or work in some of my many properties.

Let me tell you about the Thump Winter Palace. It has 16 bedrooms and 24 bathrooms. The ballroom, of course, is grandiose. Who would want it any other way? In the playroom, we have 75 video games. There is an immense theatre room with all of the sound and projection capability that anyone could want. There are 12 garages. The heated in-ground spa is a pleasant place to spend some relaxing time. There is a large bar, of course, to entertain guests. Naturally, we have walk-in closets, an automatic sprinkler, a covered balcony, and hurricane windows with impact glass (all the comforts of home).

It is my plan to invite all of the important foreign leaders here eventually. Sure, I could invite them to the White House – and that's a pretty good place to intimidate people – but this home demonstrates an even more powerful image. Maybe some thought that I simply lucked out when I won the election - that voters simply did not want my opponent in office - but one look at my Thump Winter Palace and all doubt is removed that I am not qualified to have the top job in this country.

Topic 41: Leaks

Drip, drip, drip. I'm fed up with the leaks that have caused me nothing but trouble. Here I am trying to establish an Administration that will be envied all over the world. That effort requires that the public doesn't hear any planning or any unilateral actions until I'm ready to release that information.

What is really aggravating is that the leaks have to be coming from some of my trusted staff members. Since the leaks are used to discredit my efforts not only at home but abroad, it is crystal clear that some of the leaks are coming from the Intelligence community - the FBI or the CIA or the Secret Service even.

What is the problem? I have chosen my staff carefully. They are onboard with my goals and philosophies. They are also faithful to me. They supported me during the election. Yet, here we are with leaks coming directly from one or some of the staff. It doesn't make any sense. Obviously, there has been serious disloyalty or maybe there's a mole on the staff, planted by the Democrats. I wouldn't put it past them.

As for the FBI and CIA, I haven't trusted them from the very beginning. Oh, a number of them praised me during the election, but these are probably the very guys who are not only leaking information – important security information – but are tainting the facts to make me look bad.

The leaks are going to stop even if we have to take drastic steps, maybe fire everyone and start all over. Where's J. Edgar Hoover when I need him?

Topic 42: Just What I Want

Apparently Americans have no real idea of who they elected. The United States is, of course, not a dictatorship, at least not until I came along. My Presidency is a hidden dictatorship. We call it a Democracy, but if I continue to play the cards right, no one will stop me from doing exactly what I want – not the media, not Congress, not the Supreme Court. I am the holder of the power of the President of the United States. No past President had a clue on how to maximize that power.

I will ignore the Press or let them play into my hands by trying to retaliate for my insults to CNN, the New York Times, New Yorker Magazine, whoever and whenever. I can handle Congress with a clear Republican majority and with spineless members of Congress on both sides of the aisle. I will get around the nuisance of judges all the way to the Supreme Court with Executive Orders and conventional and creative stalling. I'll confuse, amaze, and perform – all on my own.

Topic 43: My Hair Style

I've heard the snickering behind my back, again from jealous people my age who just can't believe I have this head of hair. I think that how a guy wears his hair is just as important to him as how a woman styles her hair. Veronica has been my personal hair stylist for maybe a dozen years now. She has a philosophy about it.

Me: Do you think I should change the way my hair looks, Veronica?

Veronica: Don't even think about it, Sweetie. Your hair makes a statement.

Me: I agree. Why should I look like everybody else?

Veronica: Right. It's unique. When I first created this style for you, I was so proud. And I loved that you liked it right off.

Me: It really helps that I have this kind of orange hair. That really stands out.

Veronica: Absolutely. Even if we have to touch it up a bit occasionally. That's our secret.

I know that my hair is almost a duplicate of Robert Redford's, although of course his hair is blond, but Veronica was able to give it a few twists that make my hair style even better than Redford's, in my opinion.

If a man wants to be in a power position, whether it's CEO or President, he needs to look natty and different at the same time. I think I've accomplished that with a little help from Veronica.

Topic 44: My National Security Adviser Woes

It is absolutely necessary to have a trusted National Security Adviser, usually someone who knows what's happening globally, someone who is a strategist. You would think that everyone would be anxious to have one in place. I'll tell you that it took forever, most of the first 100 days in office, believe it or not.

First, I appointed retired General Omar Hadley. The guy is a military genius. He can look at a map of trouble spots and immediately suggest military solutions. He was in the job for twenty-four hours before I had to fire him. He had been in close contact with foreign powers without consulting with me. Those discussions went back to before my election, but, oh, no, that wasn't acceptable to the public, especially the damn media. All he wanted to do was get a jump start on the job I had promised him after I became President. There was so much rain pouring down on my neck on this one with suggestions that I had encouraged him to have those meetings. Anyway, off he had to go.

Next, I came up with a three-star guy who was still in the military. Sure, he had spent most of his career in Europe, but he obviously knew how to command, ergo his three stars. Did this please everyone? Hell, no! He lasted forty-eight hours. Boom, a story of how he was totally unqualified. It seems that his entire career was in the military police. He knew all about policing our own men, an article suggested, and nothing about dealing with foreign powers. I had to admit they were right so I moved on. He was restored to his former post.

After much discussion and vetting, we went with retired General Douglas McEntyre. He lasted a week before we found out that he was a religious fanatic. He prayed all the time, morning, noon, and night. He spent more time in church than he spent in the office. We were waiting for him to come up with a basic plan to provide national security. Then we discovered his plan involved saying the Rosary. Hey, that's great if you're counting on God to do the job for you, but you have to do a little thinking yourself. I remember our conversation a few days after I appointed him to the job.

McEntyre: Mr. President, I believe that if we make the right decisions, we can not only accomplish ultimate security for our great country but we can bring peace to the world.

Me: What did you have in mind?

McEntyre: Prayer, Mr. President, prayer. If I can get in a room with some of the more influential world leaders and convince them that we can obtain that elusive serenity among nations by praying, we'll attain our goals. Maybe we can stand in the room in a large circle, hold hands, and pray.

Needless to say, he was gone a few days later.

Then I thought I'd try a woman. What the hell, I wasn't getting anywhere with the men I chose. I asked Margaret Snead if she wanted to be the National Security Adviser.

Me: How about it, Margaret, you want this job?

Snead: Not on your life. I don't want those damn Democrats poking around in my closet.

Me: What if I sweeten the deal, maybe invite you down to Boca once a month?

Snead: All right. I'll do it.

Unfortunately, she never got pass the front door. Her relationship with Paula Reed didn't help. The Press jumped all over the Snead and Reed, Who Plants the Seed thing. Not funny, especially since I didn't know about that when I asked her to serve. I thought the country would like her, being a child movie star and all.

Finally, I found someone who has been on the job for a few weeks anyway. I won't even tell you how many blew up in my face before I found Mickey Spimmane. The fact that he was a well-known author of adventure books as well as a military man didn't hurt his credentials. He's still with me despite Press efforts to torpedo him with silly innuendoes about his four wives and a mysterious disease.

Topic 45: Press Conferences

Between me and my Press Secretary, we've had it with most of the Press. I have already barred CNN, the Washington Post, New Yorker Magazine, the Albany Times-Union, and the Sun-Sentinel from sending representatives to my press conferences as well as my Press Secretary press conferences. I believe in freedom of the press and all that, but I'm told that all of these outfits have treated me unfairly in news items as well as in editorial columns.

I don't care about all those protests based on freedom of the Press. Right away I knew that the so-called journalists working for those rags were only in the room to try to make me look bad. We never called on them – we knew better – but somehow they jumped in anyway. If I pointed to someone anywhere near these guys, they would jump in as though I was calling on them. Then the questions that were asked were totally off the subjects that I wanted to cover that day. Worse than that, the questions were always veiled personal attacks on my qualifications to be President.

Press members are not only rude to me but they don't even treat my Press Secretary very well. They badger her. They don't let her get out the report of the day without interruption. They ask argumentative questions. Forget them all. I would put the gloves on with any of them right now.

Topic 46: The Russian Ambassador

I have known Pierre Kisslack for many years. As you know, he has been the Russian Ambassador to the United States for a year now. I knew him when, of course. He was a successful businessman in Russia, not to the extent that I am a successful businessman, of course, but nevertheless he had some success in a country that typically needs assistance from outside, from people such as me. I was a bit surprised when he was made the ambassador since he apparently knew very little about the United States.

Gobashitzen never told me in our many conversations, but I suspect that Kisslack was appointed immediately after the announcement of my candidacy for President. That makes sense because I believe that the Russians knew then that I would go on to win the Presidential election. Since I had worked with Kisslack very closely going back about 20 years, why not appoint a man who had some familiarity with the likely winner of the election?

Topic 47: Wiretapping

There's no question that my conversations have been taped by many, many individuals and organizations. I think it began long before I was a candidate for President but of course intensified as soon as the Democrats and other disloyal Americans believed that I was a serious candidate.

There are clear indications that the bugging was successful because no one could possibly know about some of my opinions and actions without having heard my conversations. Now, it's clear to me that I have many enemies, most of whom have been trying to torpedo my Presidency.

I took security measures to prevent bugging when I first realized that it might be happening. I hired some of the best technical people I could find to prevent this intrusion into my personal and business life. Apparently it didn't help because there is always someone who can find a way to tap into your lines no matter how hard you try to prevent it. How else would they have known about my meetings with Gobashitzen? How else would they have known about my business deals with a few governments that netted me some significant profits? How else would they have known about my secret departures from the White House in the middle of the night?

It is particularly alarming that I have been bugged not only before I was President but have had my conversations heard even after I became President.

It's not bad enough that my private conversations were heard; I was frequently videotaped also. I still can't figure out where the damn cameras were. There are such amazing technologies available these days – the bugging or the cameras could have been anywhere, the toaster, the vacuum cleaner, the microwave, who knows?

All right, so I am not totally innocent of charges that I was responsible for some wiretapping in my earlier years. Sure, I used surveillance whenever it was useful to me to do so. It all goes back to my distrust of certain employees. I wanted to know what they were talking about and whom they were talking to. That's one of the problems of being a success, especially a success when young; there's always someone who wants to shoot you down. I had to know who those people were and what their objectives were. Consequently, it made sense to have full knowledge of their activities and their plans. I arranged to plant listening devices about everywhere an employee might go, even the johns. The information I gathered was extremely useful to me. Some fired employees didn't have a clue as to how their filthy plans were exposed. Even those harmless employees who tried to pretend they were big shots by gossiping about me soon went out the exit.

Not only was it necessary for me to know about employees who were not totally faithful to me, I needed to know also if any competitors had information that would be useful to me. That meant that I had to set up an entire spy network. This setup, carefully planted in strategic locations that were primarily public but used by competitors, was especially helpful. Whenever I could make a move that provided benefit to me because I was aware of information gained in my spy network, that move was especially satisfying.

It's truly amazing how many employees and free agents wanted to participate in my endeavors to seek the truth through surveillance. I guess everyone has a little secret agent in him or her. Of course, I always rewarded the providers of information with ample rewards for their secrecy and their assistance.

Don't think I didn't use surveillance in my marriages. How else did I get sufficient information on Zina and Rachel to send them away without big pay-offs. Sure, they always insisted that they were innocent of any spousal wrongdoing, but I knew better even if I did have to interpret the information I gained through wiretapping and other forms of information gathering. I never used any of those private detectives who do that sort of work. No, I handpicked individuals who had the credentials and worked very secretly, very privately. Naturally, they were well paid.

Knowing what I know, then, about how to listen in and learn about very personal activities means that I am doubly sure that I was wiretapped by the former administration. Not everyone could spot the signals as well as I, but I sure as hell did. Maybe I can't prove it, maybe I don't have hard evidence, but I'm telling you with absolute certainty that there were ample attempts to gather information about my personal and business life before I became President.

Topic 48: Extraterrestrial Aliens

I have come to certain conclusions that are not shared by my closest confidents. Having given this very serious thought, I am convinced that what has happened to me over the past few months is clearly the work of beings outside of our planet. There is no one on Earth who could have had any success in attacking all aspects of my Presidency. There is just no one here on Earth who is smart enough to do that. There has to be extraterrestrial beings involved. I believe that these aliens are capable of mind control. That has to be the reason that high-ranking Republicans have turned against me.

This is not a new thought. I have known about aliens for a long time, but I never told anyone. Now I know how they operate. They stay out of sight; maybe they can make themselves invisible. They have definite plans to overthrow our government by taking over the minds of important government officials. I have been able to resist their efforts to capture my thinking because they can influence only dim-witted individuals. My mind is too strong to fall under their spell, but I'm sure they have been able to take over the thoughts of many Republicans, the group most susceptible to takeover.

I am considering going to Congress to ask for whatever funds we need to combat this serious threat to our government and our personal and business lives. There is a risk, of course, that members of Congress will misunderstand, probably conclude that I am imagining all of this. We had better act before it's too late.

Topic 49: Instability

Everybody's against me. When I won the election, I thought that most everyone liked me, but now I'm getting it in the neck from everyone. I don't even trust my own Vice-President. It's been a conspiracy from the start. The Press is primarily responsible. Fake facts all over the place really hurt. At first, I just ignored it all or tweeted messages that disputed what they had to say. These people never wanted me to be the President, and they've done everything they can to attack me from every angle.

I did my best to select top advisers, people in the business world who could help me run a tight ship. Somehow, they began talking behind my back. Then they got bolder, agreeing with the Press on some issues, even leaking to the Press confidential information specifically to make me look bad.

I've been accused of overreacting on issues, especially when I took the time to write a well-considered tweet. Don't they understand that this country needs a man who can make decisions without consultation with others, so we can have action on important changes?

It all started with the leaks. If I can't trust my "trusted" advisors, then I have to make decisions on my own. That might even involve decisions of war if necessary. I am capable of making those big decisions if I have to without Generals telling me what I should or shouldn't do.

I may have to retaliate against the traitors who are all around me. There will be plenty of firings soon. I just have to make whatever changes are required to get the people who will be of some help running this country, not individuals with their own agendas.

One editorial even suggested that I was "unstable." Don't they understand the pressures of running the world's most powerful country?

I am also beginning to have concerns about my personal safety. There are so many crazy people out there who want me gone. I'm starting to wonder about the Secret Service. Would they really take a bullet for me as they're supposed to do? Some of them look a bit shifty eyed, maybe not all that brave. Where does that leave me?

Just yesterday, some fool climbed over the wall around the White House. They say he wasn't armed with a gun but with a pocket knife. They can't fool me; he had a hatchet at least, I'm sure. I need to double the guard. I didn't know they would go that far to get rid of me.

Topic 50: Surprise (?) Ending

Who would have ever believed that Paul Dying and Mitch McDonald would have had the spines to participate in bringing impeachment proceedings? Worse, they led the way. They went to the Senate with an accusation about the totality of my actions. Those bastards in the Senate caved. Of course, I knew the Democrats would buy it. What really hurt is that 20 Republicans jumped in. How is that possible? I'll tell you how: They turned on me. They said my actions were dangerous to the country.

Okay, so I did chum it up with the Russians. As I explained, they're not bad guys. Did I give them information that was dangerous to our country? I certainly didn't think so, but the outpouring of anger on this subject really surprised me. One of my trusted assistants was even indicted because of this relationship with Russia. Yes, I knew that he shared information, but it was harmless, I believe, just enough to let Gobashitzen know that we're a friendly country.

Dying and McDonald called for immediate action on the impeachment, saying that the country was at great risk, in grave danger as long as I was President, something about the red button. I haven't even located that thing yet. Why couldn't they see that I was doing only what was necessary to save the country from all the dangers facing us throughout the world? How could I possibly expect that these guys would not only vote for impeachment but would lead the charge?

There they were on the floor of the House and the Senate, condemning me and my actions. At first it was just Democrats, but then a few Republicans – traitors – chimed in. The Press compared them to the valor expressed in John F. Kennedy's Profiles of Courage. Nonsense. These guys turned on their President, the man who led their party to victory at the polls.

They called me disloyal and said that our country was in immediate danger while I was in control. It wasn't just the Russian thing. The lies just kept coming – how I profited unethically while I was office (why the hell not?). How I had spotted aliens from another planet. I never said I saw them, but I knew they were there. How much proof did everyone need before we took appropriate safeguards?

They even attacked my right to tweet. I thought that tweeting was the way to reach the people directly. Some of the points I made in the middle of the night were based on facts and wisdom. Once in a while I might have said a thing or two that created quite a ruckus, but what the hell!

All right, it's over for me. I'm not waiting around for the remainder of the Impeachment proceedings. I quit. This book is going to the publisher and I'm heading for a refuge a long way from here where I can run my businesses and enjoy life. My Presidency was short and not so sweet, I'm afraid. I found out, of course, that the job of being President was a hell of a lot tougher than I thought it would be. At least this book will demonstrate that I did my best. If the country doesn't want me, then I don't want this country. I'm gone.

END

Income from the sales of this book and all books written by George A.M. Heroux goes directly to Victim Impact Speakers, a nonprofit organization that provides the following services:

Free victim assistance for anyone who has suffered a death in the family or an injury due to an impaired driver. Assistance consists of accompaniment to court, counseling, and legal advice.

Victim impact panels directed at first-time impaired drivers to help avoid recidivism and deaths and injuries that would result if the offenders continued to drive while impaired.

Presentations to high school assemblies to point out the dangers of drunk, reckless, and distracted driving.

Contributions to Victim Impact Speakers are welcome. They should be sent to Victim Impact Speakers, 4030 Thornbrook Drive, Springfield, IL 62711.

Review Requested:

If you loved this book, would you please
provide a review at Amazon.com?